How Bright the Light

Dan DeKoning

DEDICATION

This book is dedicated to my daughter Jessica.
I love you and am proud to be your dad.

After she read *How Deep the Darkness*, she called wanted to know what happened next. Although that book was meant to be a standalone, this book was born from her request to know the rest of the story.

How Bright the Light

CHAPTER ONE

Olivia Branch wheezed as she lurched down the road, careful to keep to the side, but equally careful not to step into the grass for fear of falling into the culvert. Between the pain in her leg, and her difficulty catching her breath, she doubted if she'd be able to get up again if she fell. As she walked, she held her hand pressed against her left side since it eased the ache of her battered ribs she felt each time she gasped for breath.

As she trudged on, the last of the sun disappeared from the sky.

"I'm thirsty. And tired," Olivia moaned. She stopped walking for a moment.

"Keep moving, Olivia," Daphne said.
Olivia wanted to stop and have a conversation with her ex-teacher and mentor, but in reality, Daphne wasn't there. She remained but a figment of Olivia's overactive imagination mixed with the memory of a person she once knew.

"I know, work the problem. Work the problem," Olivia muttered.

"You did it once, you can do it again," Daphne said.

Olivia had worked the problem. Only a few hours before, she'd used her ingenuity and gumption to escape captivity and subdue her captor. Now all she needed to do was find some sort of civilization and call in the calvary, and that seemed like a simple task after what she'd already been through.

In the distance, the twin headlights of a vehicle came into view. At first, Olivia felt relieved that help was close, but her pulse quickened when the thought passed through her mind that it might not be a potential savior, but rather, the boyfriend of her captor, the other half of the tag-team of terror. She looked to her left and right, to each side of the road, and realized she had no place to hide. Resigned to her fate, she stepped as far to the edge as she could and raised a hand. She waited as the lights grew closer.

With a screech of the brakes, an ancient Ford pickup truck slowed and stopped within three feet of Olivia. The driver's door wrenched open, and Olivia exhaled with relief when she saw a man who resembled a skinny Santa Claus leave the truck.

"What in the world happened to you? Do you need help, miss?"

Tears erupted from Olivia's eyes, and she nodded. "I need the police."

"Okay. I can take you. The nearest station is only twenty minutes from here."

The man guided Olivia to the passenger side of the truck and gently helped her get into the seat and got her buckled in.

"My name's Smitty," he said as he climbed in behind the wheel.

"I'm Olivia. Do you have any water?"

Smitty put the truck back in Park, jumped out, retrieved a bottle from a cooler in the pickup's bed, got back in and passed it to her. She took it and gave him a faint smile, but had to hand it back when she couldn't get it open. Smitty removed the cover and returned it to her. He watched as Olivia drank a few sips, then put the truck in gear and did a U-turn.

As Smitty drove through the darkness, Olivia slurped at her water. Once she'd downed half the bottle, she screwed the cover on it and leaned her head against the window. She didn't mean to fall asleep, but the ride in the rocking truck lulled her into a dreamless slumber.

Olivia woke when the brakes squealed, and the truck stopped. She opened her eyes, looked through the windshield, and saw a backlit sign with bright blue letters that told her they'd arrived at the sheriff's station.

Olivia undid her own seatbelt and attempted to open her own door, but she didn't possess the strength to do so. Once again, she relied on Smitty's help, and he got her out of the truck and through the front door of the building.

The deputy sitting at the front desk was on her feet the second the pair entered the room.

"What's going on here?" she asked.

"I found her walking down the middle of Mackenzie Road," Smitty said as he guided Olivia into a nearby chair.

"I'm Deputy Jameson." The deputy approached Olivia and squatted before her, so they were at eye level. When she did, the brown ponytail that almost matched her eyes shifted and landed on her shoulder. "Can you tell me what happened to you?"

Tears welled in Olivia's eyes, and she tried to speak, but couldn't. Instead, her lower jaw stayed fast.

"Do you need a doctor?" the deputy asked.

Olivia managed an almost imperceptible nod.

"What's your name?"

"Olivia. Olivia B...B...B...Branch." The dam broke, and Olivia began to wail in long, drawn out sobs. Her entire body shook as she cried, and every time she did, the pain stemming from her ribs caused an agony that only added to the tears.

"Olivia Branch?" Deputy Jameson repeated.

Olivia nodded again.

"I'll be right back," the deputy said as she stood.

She rushed back to her desk with Smitty right on her tail. The deputy searched through the papers on her desk until she finally found what she was looking for.

"Can I leave?" Smitty asked.

Deputy Jameson's eyes moved from the sheet she held to the woman sitting across the lobby.

"No, sorry, Smitty. You can't go. You need to stay here for a while."

"What? Why?"

Deputy Jameson handed Smitty the page. "Because the woman over there has been missing for weeks."

Smitty squinted at the paper and looked at Olivia. "Are you sure? They look nothing alike."

"Granted, she needs a long hot shower, but the name matches, as does the physical profile." Jameson snatched the paper from Smitty's hand. She handed him a box of tissues. "Go see if you can calm her down. In the cell down the hall, you'll find a blanket. Wrap that around her and keep her warm. I've got some calls to make."

The deputy's first call was to the sheriff, the second was to the fire department to dispatch a paramedic. Within minutes, they both arrived at the station.

Sheriff Jed Keene held the door open to allow Steve Johnson and Kara Fuentes into the station and joined Deputy Jameson at her desk to give the medical professionals room to provide Olivia with a quick examination. The sheriff watched as Steve removed the blanket Smitty had given her, and as Kara began taking and recording Olivia's vital signs. When they had Olivia lean forward so they could remove her shirt to better assess her injuries, he turned away and had Smitty do the same.

"Where did you find her?"

"Out on Mackenzie Road, Sheriff," Smitty answered. "Walking alongside the road like she was out for a stroll."

"Did she say anything to you about what happened to her?"

Smitty shook his head, his long white beard trailing a microsecond behind as he did. "Only that she needed the police and some water. She drank a bit and fell asleep while I drove here."

"Mackenzie Road? There's not much out that way."

"Nope. Beyond my place is only the quarry, and that old, abandoned farm. Not a lot going on over on that side of town."

The sheriff passed a quick glance over his shoulder and noticed Olivia had her shirt on, and Kara headed in his direction.

"How is she?" he asked as soon as the paramedic got within soft-talking range.

Kara removed the medical gloves she wore, turning them inside-out as she did and tucked them into her pants pocket. "Well, she's better than she looks. She has at the least a cracked rib, perhaps more. Can't tell if she broke any of them until an X-ray is done, but I think none are. She's got a pretty deep laceration in her leg that I stitched up. There are various scrapes, cuts, and contusions. She'll probably need a course of antibiotics. Just looking at her, I can tell she's dehydrated and in desperate need of a few cheeseburgers. She's also more in need of a shower than anyone I've ever seen."

"Can I talk to her?"

"Sure. She's pretty lucid, considering."

Sheriff Keene grabbed the deputy's chair and wheeled it over to Olivia. With an exhale, he slid into the seat and gave the woman a once over before he started speaking. He could tell she had long brown hair, but it looked like a proverbial rat's nest. It stuck out at odd angles, and where it didn't contain caked-in dirt, it looked greasy, like she hadn't washed it in at least a year. Likewise, her face was equally dirty, but her brown eyes held a sparkle that comprised the brightest part about her. Keene sniffed and realized right away what Kara was talking about. Olivia smelled of stale body odor, earth, and human waste.

Keene had experienced better smells at the county dump in the middle of an August heatwave.

"I'm Sheriff Keene. You can call me Jed. Can you give me your name?"

Olivia took a sip from the water bottle Smitty had given her and moved a matted bunch of hair from her face. "Olivia Branch."

"Do you remember your address?"

Olivia reached around, dug into her skirt pocket, and retrieved her cell phone case. She opened it, retrieved her driver's license, and handed it to the sheriff. He glanced at it briefly, then passed it over his shoulder to Deputy Jameson.

"This is your current address?"

Olivia nodded.

"Can you tell us what happened to you?"

Olivia took another drink of water. She dropped her chin to her chest and grew interested in picking at the label on the plastic bottle.

"On May fifth, I was having dinner with friends at a Mexican restaurant. I remember things got a little loud, so I stepped out for some air."

As Olivia worked on the label, the sheriff's gaze dropped to her fingers. Like the rest of her, her hands were dirty, and her nails looked worn down, cracked and chipped, like they belonged to someone who'd worked in mining for fifty years.

"I felt something sting me, like a bee. The next thing I remember, I woke up in this dark room. By dark, I mean totally pitch black. Always. They kept me as a prisoner there for, I don't know how long. I couldn't tell if it was day or night, and time stretched out like the horizon. I found a source of water and periodically got fed. At most, a sandwich, sometimes half that. Then, one day, I heard someone speaking through this pipe and I realized I wasn't the only one in there."

Sheriff Keene straightened in the chair. "Did they help you get out?"

"No. Nibbler did that."

"Who's Nibbler?"

Olivia smiled and looked up to meet Keene's eyes. "The little mouse who saved me. He'd been stealing the food I'd been rationing, and it dawned on me that he had to be getting in the room somehow, so I tied a line around him, and sure enough, he led me right to his mouse hole. Once I found that, I dug my way out. It turns out I was being held in an old silo."

"Does that deserted farm have one?" Keene asked Smitty. Smitty, who was leaning up against a wall and listening intently to Olivia's story, nodded.

"Then what did you do?" Keene asked Olivia.

"I slipped into the main house to rescue the other girl, but it turns out she and her boyfriend were the ones who took me. We had a fight, and in the end I got away. That's when Santa found me."

Olivia looked toward Smitty and nodded. Smitty gave her a half-toothless grin in return.

"May fifth you say you got taken? Are you sure?"

Olivia nodded. "Yeah. Gabby has a thing for Cinco de Mayo." She smiled, but it came out weak. Thinking of Gabby made her think of her other friends. Sarah, Michelle, Tina, and especially Heather, her best friend. "What's the date today? The twelfth? I need to get home. I have clients to tend to."

Olivia made a move to stand, but Sheriff Keene reached out and gently pushed her back into the chair. "Olivia, today is June nineteenth. You've been missing for over six weeks."

"Six… weeks?" Olivia said, with a hint of confusion in her voice. "Six weeks?" She let go of the water bottle and it dropped to the floor. It rolled for a bit and stopped when it hit the toe of Sheriff Keene's boot.

"I need to go home," Olivia said. "Can you take me home?"

Keene put his hand on Olivia's knee. "Not yet. Do you think you can take us back to the farm? Show us what happened? I realize it's a lot to ask, especially after all you've been through. We can arrest the people who did this to you."

Olivia considered it for a while, then eventually nodded. "Susie should be easy to catch. I pushed her into a well."

"A well?"

"I almost fell into it myself. I can show you where it is."

"Do you know if they're armed?"

"Susie claimed they had a gun. She said her boyfriend Michael always carries it on him. Of course, she could have lied about that too. Maybe she doesn't have any."

"Or they're armed to the teeth," Deputy Jameson added. "Maybe we should call in some backup, like the state patrol."

"There's something else. When I was going through the house, I found the IDs of other women, women that were there before me."

The sheriff looked at his deputy, then turned his attention back to Olivia. "Were there any other captives there that you saw?"

Olivia thought for a moment, then shook her head. "No. They seemed to have cameras covering all the cells, and when I looked at them, I didn't see anyone else."

The sheriff stood still for a moment, then got up and paced across the room a couple of times. He took a moment to run his fingers through his hair, then rejoined the crowd.

"Okay, here's what we're going to do. Becky, get on the phone and get the state patrol out here. I agree with you about getting some backup. And I'd really prefer not to go out there in the dark, so let's get the plan together and go in at first light. Olivia, if you don't mind, I think we'll move you into a cell where you can get some rest."

Sheriff Keene caught the look of concern that passed over Olivia's face like a solar eclipse, then quickly amended his statement.

"I'm sorry. It's the cell that we use when we need to rest and recharge. It's not really a cell. The door locks from the inside, and it has the most comfortable bed in the building. Would that be all right? I'd really like you with us when we go out to the farm."

He waited until, at last, Olivia nodded.

"I'd like you to hang around too, Smitty."

"Why Sheriff, I'd really like to get home, and you know me. I don't want any trouble."

Keene stared him down. "You're right. I do know you. I know you'd be on that redneck network of yours and everyone within a four-county radius would know what's going down within an hour. Find a seat and make yourself comfortable. We'll have you on your way as soon as we can."

Smitty grumbled something unintelligible, then stomped across the lobby and slumped down in a chair as far away from everyone else as he could.

"Until the posse gets here, there's nothing to do except wait and try to rest. Does anyone have any questions?"

Olivia raised her hand slightly.

"Yes?"

"Can I call someone to come and get me?"

Sheriff Keene nodded. "Of course. Husband? Parents?"

Olivia thought for a minute. "My friend Heather."

She opened her phone case and tried to turn on the phone. She frowned when it didn't respond. "It's dead."

"I don't suppose you have her number memorized?"

Olivia shook her head. "I barely have mine memorized."

Keene held out his hand. Olivia placed her phone in it, and the sheriff turned and handed it off to his deputy.

"Get this charged up and get it back to her."

"Will do."

"While that's happening, see if you can get contact information on her friend."

"Okay."

"But call the state patrol first."

"Okay, Sheriff, I got it."

"Great. Come on, Olivia, let's get you settled."

Olivia grabbed her water bottle and her blanket and let the sheriff lead her into the bowels of the station. She followed him down a corridor, and he stopped outside of a door with a narrow glass window in it. She expected him to use a key to open it, but the knob turned freely in his hand, and he stepped in. Olivia followed him and stopped just inside the door.

The cell walls were made of cinder block, just like all the other walls in the building, and it contained a twin bed, complete with a fluffy pillow dressed in a white pillowcase and a quilt that appeared homemade. The room also held a discarded office chair and a small table next to the cot. On the table stood a brass desk lamp and nothing else.

"Come on in. It's more comfortable than it looks."

Olivia stepped past Sheriff Keene and sat on the bed. The springs squeaked, but the mattress was thick and soft, and she could tell from the smell alone that the sheets were clean.

Keene turned on the desk light, then stepped back to the door.

"Like I said, it locks from the inside." He took a moment to demonstrate the lock, then opened the door and stepped into the hall. "You'll be safe here until it's time to leave in the morning. Try to get some rest, okay?"

Olivia nodded, and the sheriff disappeared. She went to the door and locked it. She moved to turn off the overhead light, then stopped and unlocked the door, opened it, and glanced down the empty corridor. Once the door clicked closed and she turned off the overhead, she went back to the bed, kicked off her shoes, and placed them under the bed. She snuggled beneath the quilt, closed her eyes, and for the first time in forever, slipped into a stress-free sleep.

CHAPTER TWO

Olivia woke to the sound of a gentle rapping at the door. She opened her eyes and looked toward the sound and saw Deputy Jameson peering in the small window, the light of the corridor behind her.

"Come in, it's not locked," Olivia called.

The door opened wide enough for the deputy to stick her head in.

"Is it time to go?" Olivia asked, sitting up.

"We're still waiting for the troops to assemble. I hate to wake you, but I was wondering if you'd like to catch a shower before we go."

"In the cell block? No thanks. I'll wait until I get home."

"Not here. I'll take you back to my place. It's only a half mile away. I live alone, so it'll only be the two of us."

Olivia thought for only a second before she threw the quilt back and reached under the bed for her shoes. "Thank you, deputy."

"Becky. Call me Becky. Save the deputy stuff for if I arrest you for something. I'll be out front when you're ready to go."

Olivia put on her shoes. At one point, they were a bright neon green, but now, tattered and dirty, they didn't carry a hint of what their original color was. She got herself together as well as she could and found her way to the front lobby. Although she expected it to be a hive of activity, only Becky remained in the room, sitting patiently behind the front desk.

"You ready?" Becky asked.

Olivia nodded, and Becky stood and ushered Olivia to the door. Once outside, Becky guided Olivia to a county-issued sheriff's SUV. Becky slipped it into gear, and within five minutes, she pulled into the driveway of a small ranch-style home.

"We're here," Becky said as she shut down the vehicle and opened her door.

Olivia left the SUV and followed Becky to the front door. She looked to her right and saw a face peering at her.

"I thought you said you lived alone," Olivia said.

Becky turned and spotted what Olivia referred to. "Oh, that's Molly. Don't worry about her, she's friendly. You're not allergic to cats, are you? I should have asked before I brought you here."

"No. I'm good," Olivia answered.

Becky pushed the door open, and the two entered the living room. The cat jumped down from the top of the chair it had been laying on, approached the humans, and sat at attention.

Pretty kitty," Olivia said. She reached down to pet the pure black feline with yellow-gold eyes. The cat took a sniff of Olivia's hand and bounded off to the back of the house with haste, as if its tail were on fire.

"Sorry. Usually, she's friendly. Perhaps…" Becky trailed off and let the sentence die unfinished.

"Perhaps it's because I smell like a sewer?" Olivia said.

Becky gave her a half-smile and shrugged. "Cats are sensitive to scents. Please take off your shoes."

At first Olivia got momentarily offended by the request, but it passed as Becky slipped off her shoes and placed them on a rubber mat right next to the door. Olivia placed her sneakers next to Becky's and thought they would be better off in the trash.

"Follow me," Becky said.

Olivia did, and Becky led her through the living room. They turned into a long hallway, and Becky stopped, leaned in, and flipped on a light switch. They stood in a small bathroom.

"You get ready. I'll grab you a towel." Becky disappeared down the hallway and Olivia entered the bathroom. She slipped off her skirt and let it fall and sat on the toilet to take off her socks. When she raised her arms to take off her shirt, she squealed.

"Are you okay?" Becky said, entering the bathroom with a couple of fluffy cranberry-colored bath towels in her arms.

"I can't get my shirt off," Olivia admitted.

"Ribs bothering you?"

Olivia nodded.

"I'm sorry. I argued that they should have taken you right to the hospital, but that's an hour away by car. Keene thought it better that you take us to the farm first to make the arrest and gather evidence and get your full story there, rather than sending you off to the hospital for who knows how long. I promise I'll get you there as fast as I can."

"Okay," Olivia said.

"I'll be right back." Becky left the room and returned in a minute with a pair of scissors and a small white trash bag. "The sheriff requested I collect your clothes for evidence."

Becky slipped the skirt and socks into the bag and carefully cut Olivia's shirt away from her. Becky winced when she saw the large bruises on Olivia's side. Angry bruises in colors ranging from maroon to a deep purple that spread from an inch below Olivia's armpit to two inches above her hip.

"Can you raise that arm at all?"

"Not really."

"Do you normally not wear a bra?"

Olivia thought for a moment. "It's back at the silo. I needed to use the padding, so I took it apart and never put it back on."

"Okay. Stand up."

Becky offered an arm to help Olivia stand and Becky slid off Olivia's underwear and slipped them into the garbage bag. Once naked, Becky guided Olivia over the edge of the tub.

"Can you stand there for a moment?"

"Yeah," Olivia said, although she leaned against the tiled wall for support.

Becky left the room again, and in a few minutes returned with a shower bench and another towel. The towel she added to the pile and the bench she placed in the tub. Olivia sat on the bench, and Becky removed most of her clothes except her undergarments and climbed into the tub behind Olivia and closed the shower curtain.

The shower head connected to a long hose, so Becky unhooked it and handed it to Olivia.

"Hold this. Let me know when the temperature is okay for you."

Becky turned on the water, and Olivia tested it until it reached the perfect blend of warmth.

"That's good."

Becky took the shower head from Olivia. "Hair or body first?"

"Hair. Then body. And perhaps the hair again," Olivia answered.

Becky nodded. "Perfect. Here it comes."

Becky adjusted the water pressure to a medium setting and focused her attention on Olivia's head. The water ran from the top of Olivia's skull and cascaded down her body in an almost constant stream of brown. As she watched, a few small leaves and a random twig dropped from Olivia's hair and circled the drain.

Without speaking, Becky gave Olivia's head a good rinse

and worked in a healthy amount of shampoo, massaging it in with her fingers.

"That feels so good," Olivia said. "Have you done this before?"

"Actually, yes. I worked for a couple of years at a women's penitentiary, and the number of women there who needed help bathing would surprise you. I'm going to rinse your head. Close your eyes."

Olivia did, and Becky rinsed the shampoo away. From behind her, she grabbed a washcloth and body soap and started washing Olivia's back. As she bathed her, Becky took a mental note of all the bruises, cuts, and scratches on Olivia's body. Olivia's body looked like it had been through combat, but Becky kept that comment to herself. Instead, she washed Olivia's arms and torso, then passed the cloth and soap to Olivia so she could wash her private region and legs. Afterward, Becky washed Olivia's hair a second time, this time following the shampoo with a healthy amount of conditioner and shut off the water.

Becky got out of the tub and dried herself off, then helped Olivia to the toilet and dried her. She took a plush white bathroom robe from the back of the door and wrapped it around Olivia and led her out of the bathroom and into her bedroom. There, Becky helped her into a comfortable purple chair.

"How are you doing?" Becky asked as she rummaged around in her dresser. From it, she pulled a new set of undergarments for herself and a set for Olivia.

"Everything hurts, but that shower sure helped. Thank you."

"You need a brush. Be right back."

Becky left the bedroom, and a moment later, returned. She'd slipped into dry underwear, and she carried a hairbrush and her uniform she'd left in the bathroom. The brush she handed to Olivia, the uniform she tossed on the bed. When she turned back around, she saw Olivia trying to brush her hair out with her one good arm, then took over for her.

Becky finished with Olivia's hair, then got her into a fresh pair of underwear. She offered a sports bra, but Olivia declined, not sure her ribs could take the strain. Becky got a clean pair of socks on Olivia's feet, then got her into a pair of paint-splattered sweatpants, and a Bruce Springsteen T-shirt that had seen better days.

"You literally clean up well," Becky said.

"I'm sorry I left the mess in your tub."

Becky shrugged. "A little elbow grease will clean that right up, not to worry. Now, how about some breakfast? Eggs? Toast? Juice?"

Olivia grinned. "That sounds delicious."

Becky took a moment to get back in uniform, checked herself in a mirror, and helped Olivia out of the chair.

Olivia expected to go into the kitchen next, but Becky took her back to the bathroom. Sitting on the sink was a toothbrush, still in its original packaging.

"Come join me in the kitchen when you're done," Becky said, then left.

Olivia went into the bathroom, opened the toothbrush and added a dollop of cinnamon-flavored toothpaste Becky left out for her. The cinnamon woke her taste buds, and Olivia went to work brushing her teeth, gums, and tongue before she rinsed her mouth with water and did it all over again. She finished her routine with a swish of cinnamon-flavored mouthwash, then washed out the sink and sought the kitchen.

The kitchen wasn't hard to find. Olivia simply followed her nose and the scent of frying bacon.

"You're just in time," Becky said as Olivia entered the small room. "Sit down."

Olivia took a seat at the tiny two-person table and before she'd even gotten comfortable, Becky slid a plate in front of her. Scrambled eggs, two pieces of bacon, and a slice of toast, buttered and cut into triangles, just like her mother had done a million years before.

"Don't be shy. Eat," Becky said. "Turns out I'm out of orange juice. I can offer you coffee, tea, water, or Dr. Pepper."

"Dr. Pepper," Olivia said without hesitation. She picked up her fork and dug into the eggs. She tried to be demure about it, but she couldn't help herself and within a few bites, the eggs were gone.

Next, she picked up a slice of bacon and bit into it. Becky had perfectly prepared the bacon. Not overly crisp, and Olivia moaned as she chewed.

Becky smiled as she placed a glass of soda before Olivia. "Good?"

Olivia smiled and swallowed, then took a drink of the Dr. Pepper. The carbonation set off another sensation in her mouth she'd forgotten.

"I think I want to marry you," Olivia said.

"Thanks for the offer, but I'm a registered single cat lady and intend to stay that way."

Olivia laughed and turned her attention to the toast. It didn't take long to devour the bread, and soon her plate was empty.

"You want more?" Becky asked.

"I do, but I don't think I should. I haven't eaten this much in forever."

"Oh, wait." Becky turned around and swept a couple of pill packets from the counter and handed them to Olivia. "Kara told me to give these to you to help with the pain. Make sure to take them with food."

Olivia tore open a packet and swallowed the two pills inside with the last of her Dr. Pepper. "Thanks. I needed that."

Becky checked the time. "Okay. We should probably get a move on. They'll be waiting for us at the station."

Becky took the plate and placed it in the sink.

Olivia was about to rise when a black form suddenly appeared on the table in front of her. The cat moved in closer, then nudged Olivia with its head.

"Oh, Molly. She's looking for a hug. Wrap your arms around her and give her a good squeeze, then we'll go."

Olivia embraced the cat and brought it to her chest. The cat rubbed her head under Olivia's chin and began purring.

"She's so soft," Olivia said.

"Yeah. She's also a big ham. I told you she's friendly. Molly, come here."

Olivia released her grip on the cat. Molly turned her head and saw the treat in Becky's hand. She jumped from the table and sat at Becky's feet.

"See. She's a ham, and a fickle one besides." Becky put the salmon-flavored treat on the floor, and as the cat gobbled it up, Becky made sure the kitchen was in order and turned off the lights.

"Let's hit the road."

Olivia followed Becky to the living room. Becky added Olivia's shoes to the garbage bag with her clothing and handed Olivia a pair of canvas shoes so white that the glare almost hurt Olivia's eyes.

"I'll return your clothing to you," Olivia said. "I can send it to the station or here. Just give me the address to either."

Becky opened the door. "Don't bother, you've been through enough."

Five minutes later, they were back at the station. Police cars from several agencies jam-packed the parking lot, but Olivia noticed everyone had left a spot right next to the door vacant.

Becky parked in the empty spot and turned off the SUV. "Are you ready for this? There's going to be a lot going on, and it may get overwhelming or confusing, but I'll be with you the entire time, okay?"

Olivia nodded. "Thank you. I appreciate all that you've done for me."

The pair entered the building. When they'd left, there'd been no one in the room. Now they had to push their way through the throng of uniformed men and women. As they got farther into the room, the officers noticed who was entering and made room for them to pass.

"Sheriff," Becky said as she got to the desk.

"Thank you, Deputy. Olivia, you're looking much better. How do you feel?"

"Still tired, but at least clean and fed."

"Attention!" Sheriff Keene yelled.

The room quieted.

"Our guest of honor has arrived, so—"

The sheriff stopped speaking when a spontaneous round of applause exploded from somewhere in the room that carried through like a rogue wave. Olivia's cheeks reddened from embarrassment, but she stood her ground, mainly because there was nowhere to escape to. Sheriff Keene let the clamor go on for perhaps a minute, then waved his hands to silence the room. The crowd quieted.

"As I was saying. We're ready to go. Does everyone understand their assignments?"

He paused, but no one said anything.

"I'll take that as a yes. Okay, everyone move out."

"What's my assignment, Sheriff?" Olivia asked as the rest of the officers cleared from the building.

"We have three dozen officers in tactical gear who are going to surround the place, and I've got more cops assigned to block the road in both directions. The heavy hitters will clear the area, and then we'll enter. Your assignment is to stick to Deputy Jameson. Once we get the green light, we'll bring you in to show us everything that happened. Sound good?"

Olivia didn't speak.

The sheriff put his hand on her shoulder. "Olivia, I know you don't want to go back there. Hell, I wouldn't want to either. But we need to get your story documented, and the evidence collected, so when we catch the bastards that did this to you, we'll have enough to lock them up forever."

"I'll be with you the entire time," Becky said. "Do you think you can stand me for another couple of hours?"

"Sure. I can do it," Olivia said.

"I forgot something," Becky said. Without a word, she headed to the sheriff's inner office.

"She seems to forget a lot," Olivia said.

Sheriff Keene grinned. "Don't let her fool you. She's a great deputy and smart as a whip."

The deputy appeared a second later, carrying something in her hand. "Here you go. All charged up."

Olivia looked down at what Becky was trying to hand her. "My phone? I need to call…"

"Sorry, no calls. We need to get going," Sheriff Keene said.

Dejected, Olivia slipped the phone into the pocket of the sweatpants.

Becky put her arm around Olivia. "He's right. We need a blackout for a while. We don't want the scene to turn into a circus. Besides, I talked to your friend Heather before I woke you this morning. She should be here around noon to pick you up."

At the news, Olivia felt tears well in her eyes. "Why didn't you tell me that earlier?"

Deputy Becky shrugged. "I forgot."

CHAPTER THREE

Olivia's heart rate rose as they got closer to the farm, even though she didn't recognize any of the scenery. Sheriff Keene parked on the county road, just off the driveway leading into the property, and waited. The second the digital clock on the dash recorded the half hour, the sheriff picked up the radio and asked for a status check. Olivia listened from the back seat as one unit after another checked in. Once they all did, Keene gave the go order, and the radio fell silent.

"It won't be too long of a wait here. Fifteen, maybe twenty minutes," Sheriff Keene said, looking at Olivia in the rear-view mirror.

"Are you okay back there?" Becky asked.

"Yeah. I'm good. I want to get this over with so I can go home," Olivia answered.

As they settled back into silence, Olivia stared out the window, although there wasn't much to see except tall weeds on the side of the road and the trees beyond them. Olivia, usually a patient person, became more restless as the minutes crept on.

When she felt anxious enough to scream, the radio

squelched and came to life as team after team reported in with all-clears.

"That's our cue, let's go," Keene said as he shifted his SUV into gear and pulled into the driveway.

As Keene slowly drove toward the house, Olivia kept her eye on the outside. There, she caught glimpses of officers searching the trees, not far from where Olivia herself had moved through them to get to the road.

Soon, the house came into view, and beyond that, Olivia spotted the top of the silo in which she'd spent so many horrifying days and nights. Keene parked, and he and Becky got out of the SUV. Becky opened the back door for Olivia, and Olivia stepped out.

"Find anything?" Keene asked one man nearby.

"There's no one here. Lots of disturbing things inside the house, though."

"Did you check the well? Susie fell into the well," Olivia said, pointing in the distance.

"Where?" Sheriff Keene asked.

Olivia walked through the grass, careful not to step on any of the debris in the yard. She slowed when she arrived at the edge of the well. "It's right here, underneath this trash."

Keene motioned for a couple of the troopers to clear away the debris, and once they did, the deep hole stood exposed. Keene stepped to the edge and shined his flashlight into the well.

"It's empty."

"It can't be. She has to be down there. She broke her leg."

Olivia moved to the well and peered in. "Where is she?"

"How deep was the water?" Keene asked.

"No more than six inches," Olivia said.

"Rabbit, set up a rig and get a man down there to check it out," Keene ordered.

"Yes, sir," the trooper nearest to Keene responded.

"While they're doing that, let's go into the house," Keene

said.

Someone had forced the back door open, and Keene, Becky, and Olivia entered the kitchen. There, she focused on the smashed chair she'd escaped from and took an instinctive step back toward the door.

"Are you okay?" Becky asked.

"Yes," Olivia said. She took a moment to explain what she'd gone through in the room. As she did, Becky took notes while Keene asked follow-up questions. Once Olivia told of her kitchen experiences, Keene slipped on a pair of disposable gloves and searched through the room, opening drawers, cabinets, and appliances. Olivia watched, knowing the entire time he wouldn't find anything of use.

"There are other places to spend your time if you're searching for something interesting," Olivia said. "Follow me." With Becky and Sheriff Keene on her tail, Olivia stepped out of the kitchen and into the living room. The room was a mess, its picture window shattered.

"What happened in here?" Sheriff Keene asked.

"They barred the doors, and I needed a way out, so I threw a chair through the window. When I jumped out, I got this." Olivia pointed to the large bandage covering her calf. She could tell by the seepage she either needed additional stitches or a dressing change.

Olivia passed through the living room and headed down a corridor. They stepped into a room where two troopers seemed busy collecting evidence and taking photographs.

"What do we have here?" Sheriff Keene asked.

The trooper taking pictures stopped and approached the sheriff. Her name tag said 'Redmond', and although she stood a few inches shorter than anyone else in the room, the way she carried herself made it seem as if she was the tallest.

"Well, Sheriff, this appears to be the base of operations. Each of those monitors is connected to a camera in a holding cell."

Sheriff Keene moved closer and looked at the screens. Two weren't working, but in each of the others he saw teams of troopers investigating the rooms.

"Look over here," Redmond said. "Step aside, Jim."

At her request, her partner rose from the chair he was sitting in and stepped outside the room to make more space.

Keene filled the area and looked down at the desk. Spread out before him were several wallets, driver's licenses, and a couple of college identification cards. He spotted one of interest and pointed at it. "Amanda Driscoll? Wasn't there a BOLO out on her like six months ago?"

Redmond nodded. "I've called in three of those names already, and all of them came back as missing persons."

Keene eyed the items. "There must be a dozen people here."

"It gets worse," Redmond said. She'd been standing in front of a tall, four-drawer file cabinet. She opened the top drawer and Keene looked in. It seemed filled with purses, wallets, and loose IDs. "All four drawers are full. I'm not looking forward to finding out how many people there are."

"Let's get a couple more officers in here to help you out. I want all this stuff processed efficiently. Bag all the items on the desk. Seal up the file cabinet and move the whole thing to the station. We'll deal with it there. If you find anything else like that, send it."

"Okay, Sheriff."

"Wait until I show you the next room," Olivia said.

Sheriff Keene passed her a look, then motioned for her to lead on.

Olivia took him to the next room. This one had two troopers standing guard outside the door.

"Why are you not in there processing evidence?" Keene asked, admonishing the men.

"Tell us where to start and we'll get right on it," the closest guard said.

Keene took half a step through the open door, then stopped in mid-stride. "Holy hell," he said.

Before him, the room looked dedicated to piles of clothing, strangely separated by item type. The pile of jeans and other pants was the tallest, shirts came in a distant second. Panties and bras each had their own piles as well. The only thing not in a proper pile were shoes, which seemed to be thrown against the opposite wall.

"I have a bad suspicion this isn't from a clothing donation drive," Keene said, barely audible.

"Susie said her boyfriend Michael would take all the bodies into the woods and bury them," Olivia said in a volume that matched the sheriff's.

Keene stepped back out of the room and pointed at one of the troopers. "Go to the room next door and tell Redmond to get a moving van out here. Bag up everything in here. It'll all have to go to the crime lab. After that, put in a call to the state and get some cadaver dogs up here. And get a few men to search the surrounding woods with a fine-toothed comb."

"It'll take them a year to get through all this," the trooper said.

"Probably more like two years. Now go."

The trooper left, and Olivia continued the tour, this time of the individual holding cells.

"This is where you were kept?" Becky asked.

"No. Follow me."

Olivia led the pair back to the kitchen, then outside. Keene stopped for a minute to check on the progress of the activity at the well, then Olivia took them around the house and to the silo. She noticed the heavy wood door was open, so she headed for that. She stopped, hesitant to enter.

Becky appeared at Olivia's side and took her hand. "It's okay. Take all the time you need."

Rather than wait for Olivia, Sheriff Keene stepped through

the door and into the depths of the silo. Olivia expected to see him disappear into total darkness, but for some reason, she could easily see him enter the room. He stopped somewhere near the center, then something caught his attention, and he moved off to the left and out of her sight line. Confused, Olivia took a deep breath and stepped over the threshold.

Her confusion abated when she entered the silo and discovered the team had set up a small generator and four portable lights that illuminated the entire area. Keene was talking to a colleague near the spot where Olivia had dug her way to freedom. When he spotted Olivia in the room, he made his way to her side.

"This is where you were?" Sheriff Keene asked.

"Yes," Olivia said. "When I woke up after being knocked out, I was right about here."

"Can you take us through what happened to you?" Becky asked.

Olivia gave a deep sigh, then started telling her story. As she did so, she gave Sheriff Keene and Becky a tour of the space, from the cot to the toilet pit, to the water source. She went into detail about her conversations with Susie, and how she'd misplaced her trust in who she thought was a fellow captive. She ended with the tale of how she dug her way through the silo wall and escaped. Olivia noticed that as she moved around the small space, not only did the sheriff and Becky follow her around, but so did the four other troopers assigned to the silo to collect evidence.

As she looked around at the pile of debris around the hole, she noticed her tattered bra laying on the ground. Although she held a twinge of familiarity with it, at the same time she felt like it was just a remnant of a part of her life she was more than ready and willing to leave behind.

Wrapped up in her own thoughts, she didn't even notice when a small brown blur entered the silo through her escape route. The mouse seemed just as startled as the people inside the room, and while the people all took steps back away from the rodent, the mouse ran inside the silo rather than turning around and heading back outside.

Olivia snapped out of her daydream and turned around to see what all the ruckus was. She spotted the mouse just as it attempted to hide behind one of the cot legs.

"Nibbler?"

Olivia slowly walked over to the cot and kneeled. The mouse eyed her warily.

"Nibbler, is that you, little buddy?"

Olivia outstretched her hand and held her position as still as she could. The mouse let out a squeak and moved closer to her hand. It sniffed at the tips of her fingers, and then, to the amazement of everyone except Olivia, it climbed onto her open palm and sat down in her hand.

"It is you, isn't it?" Olivia said as she stood. With a tender touch, she scratched the mouse between the ears. She rejoined the crowd of people staring at her.

"This is Nibbler," Olivia said. "He's the reason I got out. He showed me the way to the outside."

"The mouse saved you?" Becky asked.

"Sure did. And now I'm going to save him. You're coming home with me, Nibbler, and you're going to live the life of luxury. No more worrying about scavenging for food or avoiding predators for you. No way."

Sheriff Keene opened his mouth to say something, but a call over the radio interrupted him.

"Yeah, she's expected. Let her through." He smiled and turned his attention to Olivia. "Olivia, thank you for being so brave coming back here like this. I think we can take things from here. Of course, I'll be reaching out to you as we get going in the investigation, and I'm sure we'll have a lot more questions as we dig deeper. Deputy Jameson, can you take her back?"

"Are you dismissing me?" Olivia asked.

"It's not like that. Your friend is here."

"Come on, I'll escort you," Becky said.

Olivia took a step toward the door, then stopped, turned around, and gave Sheriff Keene a kiss on the cheek. "Can you do me a favor?"

"I can try," the sheriff said. "What is it?"

"Catch these bastards."

Without waiting for an answer, Olivia left the silo, this time exiting via the door with her head held high.

As they walked through the backyard, Olivia tripped over a piece of debris, but Becky was right there to catch her arm and steady her.

"Slow down a bit. Are you in pain? You're limping pretty badly."

Olivia stopped and took as deep a breath as her sore ribs would allow. "Yeah. I'm hurting a bit. I'll be okay, though."

Once Olivia had gathered her strength, she started again, having to lean more on Becky with each step.

They cleared the corner of the house, and once they stepped around a pair of patrol cars, Olivia spotted a blond-haired woman ten yards away. The woman noticed Olivia and rushed toward her. She opened her arms, fully intending to wrap Olivia in a hug, but Becky stepped in front, blocking the action.

"Careful, she's injured," Becky said, then backed away.

"Hey, Heather," Olivia said.

"Hey, Liv." Heather stepped closer to her friend and gently placed a hand on each cheek and touched their foreheads together. "I can't tell you how happy I am to see you."

"If you're so happy, why are you crying?" Olivia asked.

Heather didn't answer, but instead wrapped her arms around Olivia and gave her a light hug. Even with the light pressure, Olivia winced and grunted.

Heather tried to stop, but Olivia wrapped her good arm

around Heather and brought her closer.

"I'll leave you two to it," Becky said. "Heather, when you leave here, make sure your first stop is at a hospital. She needs proper medical attention."

"Thank you for everything, Becky," Olivia said without letting go of her friend.

"All part of the job. I hope you feel better soon. You're an amazing woman, Olivia Branch."

Becky nodded, then stepped away to give the women some room.

"Heather, can we leave now?" Olivia asked, loosening her grip.

"Sure. But you have to answer one question first. Why are you holding a mouse?"

Olivia smiled. "I'll tell you in the car."

CHAPTER FOUR

Olivia heard a key rattle in her door lock, so she got up from her seat. She took a step, kicked the edge of the side table next to the couch, and tumbled to the floor. She landed with a thud and slurred the first swear word that came to her mind. It took a moment for her to roll over, and when she did, she kicked the table leg again. The oblong table lamp teetered for a moment, looked like it would right itself, then crashed to the floor, putting a dent in the lampshade that matched the dent on the opposite side of the lamp. Olivia noticed a newly formed crack along the side and realized she'd have to dig out the black roll of duct tape and add another layer to the lamp.

"I don't know why I keep the damn thing. It doesn't work, anyway. Trash. It's going out in the trash."

Someone opened the deadbolt and turned the knob, expecting to get in, but Olivia had set the two chain locks in place. When the person tried to open the door, it swung inward only three inches before the chains tightened.

"Olivia? It's me, Heather. Are you in there?"

"Yeah," Olivia said. "Hold on."

Olivia crawled over to the couch and used it to help her get to her feet. Once vertical, she moved to the door, worked on the chains, and eventually got them free. The door opened fully, and Heather entered carrying a half-dozen reusable grocery sacks. Olivia stepped aside and Heather moved into the kitchen and placed the sacks on the counter. She selected one, opened the fridge, and started putting away the perishables.

"How are you doing today?" Heather asked.

Olivia shrugged. "Okay."

"Did you shower?"

"Almost," Olivia said.

"Almost?"

"I'm working up to it. I had other things I did."

The fridge door alarm dinged, so Heather quickly put away the milk, shut the door to silence the noise, and turned around to face her friend. Olivia had taken a seat at the kitchen island. She wore mismatched pajamas, and she'd missed a hole when she buttoned the top, so the right collar poked an inch above the left one. Her hair looked wild, like it hadn't seen a brush in at least two days, and she had a smudge of ink above her right cheek.

"Did you eat today?"

Olivia nodded. "Peanut butter and jelly sandwich."

"I could have guessed that," Heather said.

"How?"

Heather stepped around the island and pointed at a red stain in the shape of an exclamation point on the front of Olivia's shirt. She touched the jelly and determined it was dry. Probably yesterday's stain she'd overlooked.

"Did you feed Nibbler?"

"Of course I did."

Heather made her way over to the front window where Nibbler had his cage. The bedding looked fresh. He had plenty of water, and he had two small food bowls, one which contained pellets, and the other held small pieces of fresh fruits and vegetables. Heather had to hand it to Olivia. Most days she couldn't take care of herself, but she always made sure she met the needs of the little mouse. Heather didn't need to bend over to peer inside his little mouse cave, since he was sleeping on the bottom of his hamster wheel. Nibbler tended to use it more for naps than for exercise.

Heather returned to Olivia, who still sat next to the kitchen island. She had her elbow on the island and her head in her hand.

"Liv?" Heather picked up a soft snore in response. She put a hand on Olivia's shoulder and gave her a light shake. Olivia jerked awake, screamed, and kicked out. Her foot hit the island and when she pushed, she tipped back the stool she sat on. Only Heather's quick reflexes prevented Olivia from falling to the floor.

"Hey, hey. You're okay. You're home, safe and sound, and there's no one here but the two of us. Do you hear me, Olivia?"

For a moment Olivia didn't understand where she was and stared wide-eyed at Heather with no recognition in her eyes, but a few seconds later, Liv shook the cobwebs out of her head. She stopped screaming, but started to whimper, much like an injured dog. Heather took her in a tight hug and held her until Olivia's heart and breathing rates dropped into normal ranges.

"Hey, why don't we get you cleaned up? You'll feel better after a shower. Then I'll make dinner, okay?" Heather said.

Olivia slid off the stool and walked down the hallway toward her bedroom. As she took each step, Heather noticed Liv used the wall for balance. When she reached her room, she entered, and Heather followed a moment later.

"Oh, Liv. What happened here?"

Olivia looked around her bedroom. The bed was bare, the comforter and sheets lay in a pile on the floor. On top of the pile of bedding, Olivia had dumped the entire contents of her sock drawer. Rather than put the drawer back in the dresser, she'd placed it four feet away in front of the closet.

"What?" Olivia said.

"What went on here? Were you looking for something?"

Olivia glanced around the room and presumably spotted nothing out of order. "I don't remember."

"Okay. Let's get you in the shower."

Olivia didn't answer. Instead, she pushed her pajama pants down in one smooth motion and stepped out of them. When she tried to remove her shirt, she didn't have the dexterity to undo the misaligned buttons. Heather turned her around and unbuttoned the top, then Olivia shook it free and let it fall onto the pants. If Olivia had any problem standing stark naked in front of her friend, it didn't show.

"You need any help getting in there?" Heather asked.

Olivia shook her head, then turned to walk to the bathroom. As she pivoted, Heather spotted the ugly scar where Olivia had endured the surgery to have titanium plates added to two ribs. Even though six months had passed, Heather still hadn't gotten used to the sight of the imperfections on Olivia's normally perfect body.

Once Olivia was out of sight, Heather retrieved the discarded sock drawer and started throwing the scattered socks into it, not bothering to fold anything nice, or even to take the time to match any pairs. Heather had noticed several changes in Olivia's personality over the last few months, one of them being Olivia no longer paid any attention to the way she dressed. If she wore matched socks these days, it was most likely an accident, and there were occasions when Olivia wore a sock on one foot but not the other.

After Heather got most of the socks back in the drawer, she shoved it back into the dresser. Next, she turned her attention to the pile of bedding. She picked up the sheets first, and when she did, a pile of crumbs cascaded from the fabric to the floor like a snowfall. Not wanting to put them back on the bed, she crumpled them into a ball and carried them into the laundry room. On the way back to Olivia's room, she stopped at the hall closet and retrieved a fresh set.

It didn't take long to make Olivia's bed, and once the sheets were on, she picked up the comforter. She gave it a good shake to remove the crumbs, and when she did, she heard a thunk and glanced at the ground just in time to see something rolling out of sight. Heather dropped the blanket, got on her knees, and peered under the bed. She reached, and from the darkness, she extracted a bottle. She didn't need to rotate the bottle to read the label to guess what it was. Vodka.

Heather lay on her stomach to get a full view but saw nothing else under the bed except a sock and a T-shirt covered in dust bunnies. She stepped to the dresser and searched through every drawer except the sock drawer, not really concerned if it looked like she'd rifled through them.

In the closet, she found what she expected to find. Way in the back, shoved inside a cowboy boot, was another bottle. The dark liquid she couldn't identify on sight, but once she got it into the light of the room, she discovered it was a half-full bottle of brandy.

Heather took both bottles into the kitchen, dumped the contents into the sink, and left the apartment long enough to take a quick trip down the hallway and drop the bottles into the garbage chute. When she returned to the apartment, she did a quick look through the kitchen but found no other evidence of Olivia's newfound love for booze.

Heather sat down on the stool Olivia had almost fallen out of, pulled her cell from her back pocket, and selected a number from her contacts. On the third ring, it connected.

"Hey," Gabby said when she answered the call. She wasn't much for greetings.

"Hi, Gabby. I think we've got a problem with Liv. I found alcohol in her bedroom."

There was a pause on the end of the line, and Heather looked at the display screen, wondering if the call had disconnected. The timer kept advancing, so she figured Gabby still had to be there.

"How long has she been drinking?" Gabby asked.

"To be honest, I don't couldn't tell you. Most days, she seems completely normal. Well, normal for her. She still has a lot of anxiety and never wants to leave the apartment. I'm here every day, so I think this may have been an ongoing thing that has ratcheted up. I don't know."

"Does she have any symptoms?" Gabby asked.

"Like what?"

"When my dad was at his worst, he'd have blackouts, aggression, anxiety, coordination issues, hand tremors, slurred speech. Those sorts of things."

"Other than the anxiety, I don't think so, although she seemed to have some coordination and balance issues when I got here a while ago."

"How long was she on the pain meds for her ribs?"

Heather pondered for a moment. "I think it was supposed to be for two or three weeks, but somehow she stretched it out to a couple of months."

"Does she have any drugs around the house?"

"Beats me. I'd need to check. When I checked the bedroom, I didn't find anything other than the alcohol, but I'd have to search the rest of the place."

"Make it a good search," Gabby said. "And don't just look for prescription bottles. She could very well have some pills stored in a sandwich bag or an envelope. How's she doing with her day-to-day activities?"

Heather told Gabby that Nibbler seemed well taken care of, but Olivia seemed to have difficulties caring for herself.

"Where did she get the booze if she's not leaving the house?" Gabby asked.

"I have no clue. I know I didn't bring it in."

"Could she have had it delivered?"

"Hold on."

Heather set the phone on the island and searched the living room for Olivia's phone. She found it right away on the floor next to the lamp that had taken a beating. Heather placed the lamp back on the table and picked up the phone. She returned to the island and retrieved her own cell.

"I'm back. Let's see what we have here."

First, Heather looked at the app list on Olivia's phone. "There are no delivery apps on here at all, not even for pizza."

"Any calls to or from people you don't recognize?"

Heather checked the incoming and outgoing call logs and the texts. "No. Just from our core girl group, and some of Olivia's family members."

"Huh. I don't know what to tell you. Perhaps you should ask her where she got it."

"How do you think that would go over?" Heather asked.

"The only way to find out is to ask her. She could get angry, or lie to you about it, or deny the whole thing. It was like that with my dad. Whenever confronted, he'd gaslight whoever he was talking to."

"Okay. I'll ask her about it over dinner tonight. Hopefully she'll tell me the truth. I'd better go. She'll be out of the shower soon, and I need to get dinner on."

"Call me back if you need me."

"Thanks Gabby. Later." Heather ended the call and placed her phone next to Olivia's. Heather got up from the stool and opened the fridge. She'd packed it with groceries, and had several options for dinner, but decided the easiest would be to pan fry a couple of burgers and throw some tater tots into the air fryer. It wasn't gourmet, but it technically qualified as dinner.

Heather bent over to retrieve a frying pan from the lower cabinet next to the stove, and when she stood, Olivia was standing right behind her. Startled, Heather dropped the pan, and as it clattered on the floor, Olivia took two steps back and covered her face with her hands.

"I'm sorry. Heather, I didn't mean to scare you. I didn't know what you were..."

"Hey, Olivia, it's okay," Heather said. She reached out a hand and gently touched Olivia's arm. She guided her to the stool and sat her down.

"Do you want something to drink? Juice? Water? Dr. Pepper?" Heather asked.

"I'll take some water."

Heather nodded, retrieved a plastic cup from the cupboard, and filled it from the fridge. She placed the cup in front of Olivia, and Liv picked it up with two hands and drank. Heather retrieved the pan from the floor, gave it a quick wash in the sink, and placed it on the stove.

"Burgers and tots okay with you?"

Olivia gave a slight smile. "Yeah. Sure. Sounds good."

Heather grabbed a package of ground beef from the fridge, opened it, pulled off a handful and began forming it in the shape of a patty.

"Are you feeling better after your shower?" Heather asked.

Olivia nodded. "Much."

"You look better. Can I ask you about something?"

"Sure thing."

Heather wasn't sure how to approach the subject, then decided to go with a direct one. "Why did you have the alcohol in your bedroom?"

Olivia took a sudden interest in her water glass and looked down into it like there was something swimming in there.

"You're in a safe space here, Liv. This is your home. I'm your friend. You can tell me."

"Your burgers are smoking," Olivia said.

Heather turned around and saw she'd set the heat too high. "Oh, crap." She turned down the heat and turned on the vent fan above the stove. She dug a spatula out of a drawer and flipped the patties. "I think they'll be okay. Besides, a little crunch never hurt anyone."

"I've been having trouble sleeping," Olivia said while Heather's back faced her.

"I understand," Heather said. She'd spent many nights at Olivia's house, curled up in bed with her friend. Although she tried to stay awake while Olivia was, she eventually ended up falling asleep. At first, she felt guilty about it, but logic set in, and Heather knew she still needed to live her life. She had work to go to each day, errands to run, and her own apartment to maintain.

"Where did you get it?" Heather asked. "I didn't think we had any here."

"From Mr. Everett."

"The widower down the hall?" Heather asked.

Olivia nodded. "A few days ago, I thought I'd go down and check my mail. Like you suggested. Baby steps, you know. Like taking the garbage out and taking care of Nibbler, right?"

"That's right."

"When I came back from the mailbox, Mr. Everett was entering his apartment. I told him we were having some people over and asked if he had any alcohol lying around he didn't want, and he gave me two bottles."

"Whiskey and gin?" Heather asked.

"No. Brandy and vodka," Olivia answered without pause.

Heather smiled, satisfied that Olivia was telling the truth. She just needed to have a talk with Mr. Everett.

The air fryer beeped, and Heather exhaled, satisfied for the moment. "You think you can rescue those tots and get some plates out for us?"

"Yeah," Olivia said.

Dinner turned out to be the highlight of the day for both of them. When Heather added a ketchup smiley face to the burgers she served, Olivia let out a genuine laugh, a laugh Heather hadn't heard in months. Then they spent an hour talking about random things, just like old times. Olivia even helped with the dishes, and afterward they settled on the couch and watched an old Tom Hanks movie.

At one point, Heather looked over and caught Olivia with a wide yawn.

"Are you tired?" Heather asked.

"I think so. Can you stay with me?"

"Of course." Heather found the remote and turned off the television. "Let's get ready for bed."

Olivia got up and headed for the bedroom while Heather followed behind and made sure she secured the door locks and turned off the lights. The hallway light she left on, and from the hall closet on the shelf above the sheets, she retrieved her own set of pajamas. She went into the bathroom, changed, and brushed her teeth. By the time she got to the bedroom, Olivia was already under the sheets, on the side closest to her, facing the door.

Leaving the hall light on, Heather closed the bedroom door as she entered, then walked around the bed and got to her side. From the drawer in the bedside table, she extracted a heavy sleep mask and put it on, since Olivia always insisted on sleeping with the lights on.

"Good night, Olivia. I'll see you in the morning."

Olivia didn't respond, so Heather rolled over and put a gentle hand on Olivia's side. By touch alone, Heather could tell Olivia had already drifted off to sleep, and Heather whispered a prayer that Olivia could rest easy for once, free of the nightmares and terrors that seemed to plague her each night.

CHAPTER FIVE

Heather let herself in with her key and found the kitchen and living room devoid of anyone. To her surprise, both areas were clean, and there was something different about the space that she couldn't quite put a finger on, so she stood still and let her eyes search out the difference.

After a moment, she realized what it was and snapped her fingers. "The Frankenlamp is gone. Olivia? Where are you?"

"I'm in the bathroom," Olivia called out from the depths of the apartment.

Heather walked down the hallway, stopping long enough to glance into Olivia's bedroom. She'd made the bed and straightened things a bit. A couple of clothing items sat outside the laundry basket instead of in it, but Heather took it as a win overall.

"Are you about ready to go?" Heather said.

"Do I have to? I think we should stay in. Wouldn't it be better to order in a pizza and stay here?"

Heather entered the bathroom and sat on the tub side. "How's it going in here?"

"Okay, I guess. I can't get my hair right." Heather watched as Olivia tipped her head forward, brushed it out, then threw her head back and bundled it all in a ponytail. A strand slipped free and curled around onto her cheek. Frustrated, Olivia ripped the ponytail from the elastic band and repeated the process.

Heather watched as Olivia fixed her hair and fixed it again. She checked the time on her phone, rose and held out her hand. Olivia placed her brush in Heather's waiting palm and turned around so Heather could round up all the stray hairs and place them neatly in the ponytail. That done, Heather placed the brush on the sink and ushered Olivia out of the bathroom.

"Do I look okay?" Olivia asked.

Heather gave her a once over. Olivia wore blue jeans and a dark green sweatshirt. Another change in Olivia's personality. Heather made it a point to drag Olivia out of the house at least twice a month, and Olivia's cute skirts, sundresses, and even leggings stayed sequestered in the closet. Olivia would wear T-shirts around the house, but when they left the apartment, she bundled up, showing at most only her hands, neck, and head.

Olivia let loose a long sigh. "Let's get out of here if we must."

Olivia stopped on the way past her bedroom and grabbed a baseball cap from the doorknob and put it on. Together, the women left the apartment, and Olivia stopped long enough to secure each of the locks on the door.

A few minutes later, they were in Heather's Subaru, speeding through the streets of the city. Heather's new SUV had lane assist, and she had some difficulty paying a hundred percent attention to the road, so every time she crossed the center line or got to close to another car, her SUV would erupt in a string of beeps until she centered in her own lane.

Each time the car beeped, Olivia tightened her grip on the door handle, expecting a fiery crash at any second.

Heather looked over at her friend and noticed Olivia's tense stature. "Would you relax? We're going to be fine."

Olivia passed Heather a brave smile, then feigned relaxation so Heather would pay attention to the road instead of her.

Heather slowed to a stop at a red light, and when she stopped, Olivia looked across the road and spotted Garcia's Cantina. To anyone else, it was only a restaurant that specialized in run-of-the-mill Mexican food. To Olivia, simply the sight of it sparked a full-blown panic attack.

"Go, Heather, drive!" Olivia screamed.

"What?"

Heather looked over at Olivia, who was practically standing in her seat, frantically pointing at the road ahead.

"Drive. Go, Heather!"

"Liv, I can't. It's a red light."

Olivia glanced at Heather, then at the stop light above them. She looked to the left and right and noticed no cross traffic coming. She leaned across Heather's lap and used her hand to press down on the gas pedal. At first Heather resisted with the brake, but Olivia punched her in the knee and Heather let up the pressure for a moment. The white Subaru lurched forward, and since Olivia wouldn't let up on the gas, Heather had no choice but to run the light and steer the car. After they passed a few blocks, Olivia let go of the gas pedal and Heather pulled into the first parking lot they came to and slammed on the brakes.

"Jesus, Olivia, what was that about? You might have killed us!" Heather tried to corral the anger in her voice but failed.

Olivia looked at Heather, then opened the door. She wanted to get out but got wrapped in the seatbelt. She struggled to release it for a few moments, but finally got it free, left the Subaru and began walking small circles in the restaurant's empty parking lot.

"Aw, hell," Heather said. She turned off the car, exited, and rushed after her friend. She looked ahead and saw Olivia was still walking in circles but had made it almost to the opposite side of the parking lot. Heather jogged to her friend and grabbed Olivia by the elbow to stop her.

"Olivia, stop."

Olivia tried to squirrel away, but Heather interlocked her arm into Liv's and planted her feet. Liv tried to break free, but since Heather outweighed her by twenty pounds, Olivia couldn't get away. Unable to break free, Olivia fell to her knees and began sobbing into her hands.

Heather crouched and hugged Olivia. Rather than say anything, Heather let Olivia cry it out for a while. Once the sobbing stopped, Heather helped Olivia to her feet and guided her back to the car. Olivia sat in the passenger seat sideways, her feet dangling outside.

Heather took a few deep breaths and buried her ire deep down inside so she would treat her friend with a soft touch rather than like someone who would have potentially gotten them both killed, or even worse, a traffic ticket for running a red and extremely reckless driving. "Want to talk about what happened?" Heather asked.

Olivia wiped her face on the sleeves of her sweatshirt and searched around for a tissue. Heather retrieved a few napkins from the glove box, and Olivia used those to blow her nose and further clean her face.

"I saw that place, and it spurred something in me. I had to get away from there."

"What place?"

"Garcia's."

"Oh, crap, I'm sorry, Liv. I should have known better than to drive past there. We were running late, and I got on autopilot, and that's the quickest route to the coffee shop. It's my fault."

Olivia sniffed and wiped her nose again and crumpled the napkin into a small ball and placed it on the floor.

"No, Heather. I shouldn't have reacted like that. It seems I need to learn how to deal with things like that. I can't be afraid of everything forever."

Olivia reached into the front pocket of her jeans and extracted a small, single-shot-sized bottle of vodka. Before Heather could react, Olivia uncapped the bottle and drank the contents without hesitation.

"Give me that!" Heather said, reaching for the bottle.

Since Olivia had already drained it, she handed over the empty container.

"Where did you get this?" Heather asked.

Olivia's tears came back. "I'm sorry, Heather. I needed it."

"Olivia."

Liv grabbed another napkin and dabbed at her eyes, more so to hide her face than to catch her tears.

"Do you have more of these at home?" Heather asked.

Olivia nodded.

"Where?" Heather got into the position of the stern schoolteacher waiting for an uncooperative student to give up the erasers they'd been throwing across the classroom. She stood with hands on hips, head lowered, a scowl on her normally peaceful face.

Olivia relented and told her, and Heather turned around, took a few steps away, and made a quick phone call. When she finished, Heather got Olivia righted in the SUV, secured the seatbelt, and climbed back into the driver's seat.

"You good to go?" Heather asked.

"Yeah," Olivia said without turning from the passenger window.

The pair traveled in silence and eventually Heather pulled into the parking lot of a coffee shop and parked. Inside the plate-glass window, she spotted Tina and Michelle sitting opposite each other, almost directly in front of the SUV. Tina turned, spotted Heather, and waved. Heather nodded in return.

"Hey Olivia, check it out."

Olivia looked up and glanced in the window and noticed her two friends.

"They're waiting for you. Come on."

Heather and Olivia left the car, and Heather held the door open to the shop while Olivia walked in before her. By the time they got to the table, Tina and Michelle were already standing and waiting to greet their old friend.

"Liv," Tina said, and she wrapped Olivia in a bear hug. "It's been too long. I'm so happy to see you!"

"Me too," Michelle said, wrapping her arms around both women. "It's been, what, months?"

"Do you remember us coming to visit you in the hospital?" Tina asked, letting go and allowing Olivia to catch a breath.

"Sit down and stay a while," Michelle said, sliding back into the booth.

Tina slipped into her spot, and Olivia sat next to Tina.

"Hospital?" Olivia said. "No, I don't remember that."

"You were pretty out of it," Michelle said. "I'm not surprised. We came to visit a few times."

"Hey," Heather said, interrupting, "I'm going to use the bathroom. I'll be right back. Order me a cup of orange tea, will you? With honey?"

Heather left the women to their small talk, backtracked to the door, and slipped out of the coffee shop. She'd seen Gabby pull into the parking lot, and rather than take the open spot right next to Heather, Gabby parked on the far side of the lot where no one could spot her from the restaurant windows.

"Did you find it?" Heather asked as Gabby got out of her bright red Ford Mustang.

"Took me a minute, but yes, I did."

Gabby opened the trunk and picked up a box of powder laundry detergent and handed it to Heather. Heather took the package and opened the top. When she looked in, she saw what she expected to, which was a bunch of white powder with patented blue stain-release crystals.

"What's this?"

Gabby took the box from her, bent over, and dumped the powder onto the concrete. She removed a piece of cardboard that acted as a tray to hold the powder and handed the box back to Heather.

"It's a whole bunch of clever is what this is," Gabby said.

Heather looked inside the box again and this time she saw a bunch of travel-sized bottles of alcohol. "I was afraid of this. Did you find any others?"

Gabby shook her head. "Not in the limited time I was at the apartment. The way she hid this, we'd have to do a thorough search of the place. I'm talking about looking inside the air vents, checking out the toilet tank, and every other nook and cranny where she could hide these things. She needs help, Heather. I know you're doing your best, but honestly, Olivia needs a professional."

"How did you even find these?" Heather asked.

"Even though she told you to check the laundry, I got lucky. She'd spilled some detergent, and I noticed the box wasn't closed all the way. When I went to shut it, I spotted the fake bottom."

"Impressive catch." Heather took one bottle from the box and slipped it into her pocket.

"You'll take care of these?" Heather asked.

Gabby nodded, then set the box back in her trunk and slammed it shut. "You'll never see these again."

"Okay. Let's go in."

Gabby followed Heather into the coffee shop and as they approached the table, they noticed Sarah had arrived.

"See who I found?" Heather said as she sat next to Sarah.

Gabby leaned over and gave Olivia a hug and a kiss on the cheek before she sat next to her. "It's good to see you, Liv."

A waitress appeared with Heather's tea. While she was there, she took orders from anyone who didn't have something, then hurried away to fill the orders.

Heather sat back, added a dollop of honey to her tea, and

stirred it while she listened to the small talk around the table, which mostly involved peppering Olivia with questions, which she answered. Except when Sarah asked. Judging by Olivia's body language, Heather could tell that Olivia was having a tough time, and that although she remained polite toward Sarah, she seemed distant from her at the same time. Sarah, at some point, caught on to the same thing because fifteen minutes in, she stopped taking part in the conversation and only nodded along, or talked when she was directly spoken to.

When the conversation trailed off, Heather cleared her throat. Since she exaggerated the sound and motion, everyone at the table stopped what they were doing and looked at her. She reached across the table and took one of Olivia's hands in her own.

"Olivia. Everyone at this table loves you and cares about you. We're all friends here."

Olivia glanced from face to face and locked eyes with everyone for a few seconds, except for Sarah.

Olivia smirked. "Oh shit, is this an intervention?"

"It wasn't supposed to be," Heather said. "But I'm worried about a few things."

"Like what?"

"Like we never see you," Tina blurted. "Don't you like us anymore?"

Olivia's eyes dropped to the table, and she took a sudden interest in playing with a spoon. "Of course I like you. I've just been… busy."

"Are you back at work?" Gabby asked.

"No. But I plan on taking on clients again soon. Several of my old ones said they're waiting to work with me."

"Have you been talking to anyone?" Tina asked.

"Of course. I talk to Heather every day. And Nibbler."

"Who's Nibbler?" Michelle asked Sarah.

"Her pet mouse," Sarah whispered back.

"I mean, have you really talked to Heather about everything you went through?" Tina asked.

Olivia concentrated on the spoon. She pushed the end of the bowl, and the spoon popped up in the air, came down on the table, then toppled over the edge. Having nothing more to play with, Olivia folded her arms to her chest.

"Has she, Heather?" Tina asked, redirecting her question.

"No. I've asked, but I didn't want to push her too far or too fast. And now I'm worried about this."

Heather reached into her pocket, extracted the small bottle, and placed it on the table in front of her.

Olivia glanced at the bottle, then leaned forward. "Where did you get that?"

"You know where. Olivia, why?" Heather said.

Olivia snapped her arm forward as quick as a cobra strike and grabbed the bottle. No one made a move to stop her.

"Look. None of you could possibly understand anything about what I went through. What it was like. What I had to suffer through!" Olivia raised her voice as she spoke, and several other patrons around the coffee shop looked up to see what the disturbance was. "And I need a little help dealing with things sometimes, or I need help sleeping. So, I have a little drink. It's not a big deal. Lots of people do it. And I can stop any time I want. I don't need this. I just want it." Olivia waved the little bottle of vodka in the air, then threw it down on the table. It bounced once, then disappeared into the space between Heather and Sarah.

"Olivia, please. Calm down," Gabby said.

"I am calm!" she screamed.

More eyes from the area stared at her, and their waitress made a few steps toward the booth, then stopped, undecided of whether to get involved.

"I'm leaving," Olivia announced. She got up from the booth, walked four paces toward the door, then tripped over a chair leg and fell to the ground.

Heather was out of the booth in an instant and arrived at Olivia's side just as the woman sitting at the table near where Olivia fell stood and helped Liv into a chair.

"Are you okay?" the woman asked.

"I'm fine," Olivia spat.

"Somehow, I can't believe that. I've overheard what you're going through, and I'm pretty sure I can help you."

"Who are you?" Olivia asked.

"Trish Longstreet. I'm a psychiatrist." She opened her phone case and pulled out a business card. She handed it to Olivia. "I primarily deal with people who have suffered traumatic experiences and help them work through things."

"You don't know what I've been through," Olivia said.

"I know. But I also know what signs to look for in people, and from what little I've observed, you're displaying several of them. Look, if you don't want to talk to me, that's fine, but like your friends said, you need to talk to someone. For your own sake."

"Thanks, but no thanks," Olivia said.

Before anyone could say anything else, Olivia stormed out of the coffee shop.

"I'm sorry about that," Heather said. "She's had a tough time lately."

"I can tell," Trish said. "What's your name?"

"Heather. That was Olivia you just met."

"Take this," Trish said, handing Heather the business card. "My office isn't too far from here, and I've got an hour free at two. Do your best to bring Olivia by, and we'll come up with a plan to get her back on the right path."

Heather took the card and looked at it for a second. She nodded, then followed her friend out to the parking lot.

CHAPTER SIX

At a quarter to two the next afternoon, Heather and Olivia stood outside of a brownstone building. Heather looked at the list of tenants on the mailbox and found T Longstreet assigned to a first-floor office.

"Are you ready for this?" Heather asked.

"I don't know. I think you're right, though. It probably won't hurt."

"Let's go in." Heather opened the door and motioned for Olivia to enter first.

Olivia did and opened the first door to her right and stepped into an outer office. There was a desk there, but no one was present. There were two closed doors on opposite ends of the room and two leather-covered chairs. Olivia slid into one, and Heather hovered for a second, then sat down in the second.

"Are we still early?" Olivia asked.

Heather pointed at a clock on the wall. "If that's the right time, ten minutes yet."

A door opened and Heather and Olivia both looked to their right. A twenty-something man wearing blue jeans, with a button-down shirt and tie, entered the room.

"Hi. Sorry. Nature called." The man moved behind the desk and clicked a couple of keys to kill the screen saver on his computer. "Do you have an appointment?"

"This is Olivia Branch. She has a two o'clock," Heather said.

The man clicked a few more keys, frowned, then shook his head. "I'm sorry. I don't have anyone scheduled for two. Do you have the correct day?"

"We met the doctor yesterday, and she recommended we come in. She said she had an open hour."

"Oh, wait." The man searched his desk and, after a moment, pulled a pink sticky note from his desk. "Olive, at two," he said, holding up the note. "That must be you. Sorry about that. Trish gave me this an hour ago, and I forgot all about it."

The other door opened and an elderly man wearing a tweed coat and carrying a cane stepped through the waiting room and left the door without speaking to anyone.

"I'll be ready for you in a minute," Trish said, sticking her head out the door.

Olivia shifted in her seat twice.

"Do you want me to go in with you?" Heather asked.

"Do you want to?"

"Sweetie, that's totally up to you. If you don't want me in your business, that's fine. If you want me with you, that's good, too, provided the doctor is okay with it."

"Maybe I'll do this first session myself and see what it's like."

Heather grabbed Olivia's hand and gave it a squeeze. "Good."

The receptionist's phone buzzed once, then stopped.

"She's ready for you," he said.

Olivia stood, took a few steps to the door, then turned around and glanced at Heather.

"I'll be waiting right here," Heather said.

Olivia smiled, then walked into the inner office, closing the door behind her.

On the far wall in front of the windows stood a large wooden desk, behind which the doctor sat. Before the desk stood two chairs, twins of the ones in the outer office. To the left was a row of file cabinets, and to Olivia's right was a leather couch.

"Where should I sit?" Olivia asked.

"Wherever you would feel the most comfortable."

Olivia moved to a chair by the desk, bypassing the couch. Dr. Longstreet stood, made her way around the desk, and sat in the chair next to Olivia.

"You don't look much like a doctor," Olivia said.

Trish smiled. "I guess not."

Like the receptionist, Trish wore blue jeans with a teal blouse in a style that seemed more casual than dressy. On her feet were a pair of socks that matched her blouse. Olivia assumed the shoes lay on the other side of the desk.

"I've found in my practice I get better results if I present myself more casually."

"What if you have someone who prefers someone more professional?" Olivia asked.

Trish smiled. "I have several colleagues who take on a variety of clients who come to see me. Some people do like a more clinical psychiatrist. Some people prefer a male doctor over a woman. In my field, the most important part of the treatment is to make sure that the client is comfortable."

"What should I call you?" Olivia asked.

"You can call me Dr. Longstreet or Trish. Or Doc. Anything is fine with me."

Olivia stared at the doctor for a moment. Trish had hazel eyes and long eyelashes. She had light olive skin, similar to the cultures that bordered the Mediterranean, and the long dark hair on her head had a slight curl to it.

"So now what?" Olivia said.

"How about we start by telling me about yourself?" Trish

said.

"Like what?"

"Whatever you'd like to share. Tell me about your childhood, or your parents, or your job. Whatever you feel comfortable telling me. This first session is really just about us getting to know each other."

Olivia stood silent for almost a full minute. "Well, I was born in October…"

***

Detective Gloria Torres was considering leaving for the day. After all, she'd already put in a forty-hour work week, and she was only three days into her shift. She was hungry, irritated, and was working on a migraine for the ages. Her desk phone rang. She had half a thought of walking away and pretending she didn't hear it, but instead, she picked it up.

"Detective Torres." She listened to the caller for a moment. "Okay. I'll be there in twenty."

Torres grabbed her jacket, put it on, and headed down to the patrol car that was waiting outside the precinct for her. Eighteen and a half minutes later, they pulled into the city cemetery.

"Where are we headed?" the driver asked.

"Follow this road around to the back and look for all the other cars," Torres said.

The car climbed a hill, and once it crested, Torres could see the crowd gathered a few hundred yards away. Besides the three cop cars, there was a hearse parked nearby, the cemetery's work truck, and the medical examiner was moving up the road just ahead of them.

Once on scene, Torres exited the car and asked the first patrolman for the story, but he directed her to the cemetery caretaker.

"What's the story here, Clark?" Torres asked.

"How'd you know my name?" he asked. Clark looked like every other cemetery worker Torres had ever seen. He wore a long-sleeved green shirt under dark brown overalls. There were patches of dirt on both knees. If he turned around, Torres suspected he'd have a plaid handkerchief shoved into his back pocket.

"The patch on your overalls," Torres said, pointing to the center of the man's chest. "So, I ask again. What's the deal?"

"Doing a burial and have a body," Clark said. He took a moment to turn his head and spit into the grass, half of it landing on his right boot.

"Isn't that what's supposed to happen?" Torres asked.

"The body I'm supposed to plant is in there," he said, pointing at the hearse. "The one that ain't supposed to be is already in the hole."

Torres looked over at the burial plot. Around the edges was fake grass, and chairs were set up underneath a portable canopy, ready for a funeral. She stepped up to the edge of the hole and looked in. There, in the grave's bottom, was a woman lying face down in the vault.

"See?" Clark said as he stepped to the detective's side. "She ain't supposed to be."

"What time is the funeral?" Torres asked.

Clark dug an old-fashioned pocket watch from his overalls. "Two hours from now."

"Not if we're not done in time. You got a ladder?"

"Uh-huh."

"Good, go grab that for me."

"I suppose you want me to climb down there?"

Torres turned around to see who was speaking to her. "Well, hello, Doctor Jimmy. I thought you were on vacation."

Dr. James Seer, Assistant Medical Examiner, stepped up to the grave and looked in. "Got back a couple of days ago."

"Where did you go? New Jersey, I heard."

"Close, Detective. Singapore. For my honeymoon."

"Oh, that's right. How is the new love of your life? Is she sick of you yet?"

"Don't be jealous, Gloria. You had your chance. Sorry, but you missed out on all this."

Clark returned with the ladder and slid it into the grave. "That ain't no way to talk to no lady," he said to Seer.

Torres smiled. "It's okay, Clark. The doctor and I go way back to the old neighborhood. We even dated for a while. When was that?"

The doctor shifted his hat on his head, then checked the ladder to make sure it seemed secure. "As I recall, it was for a week in the fifth grade. You need me in a full suit on this one?"

"No. You can go down as is. There's no way she got killed down there. It has to be a random body dump. I'll send a tech down there after you get her out."

Without further fanfare, the doctor swung his leg over the ladder and started his quick descent. As he got closer to the bottom, he stopped on the lowest rung and inspected the concrete vault that would eventually hold the body that was supposed to be there.

"There are no footprints or anything here. I think you're right and someone dropped her in. Send down my camera, will you?"

Torres turned and looked at the gear the doctor had carried to the site. Sitting on top of a black backpack was a high-end digital camera. She grabbed it and lowered it over the edge.

"Thanks," Seer said as he took the machine.

Still standing on the lower rung, he snapped off several shots of the area, including the space around the body and the body itself. Satisfied he had what he needed from that angle, he stepped into the vault and took more shots of the body from different positions.

"It looks like she got thrown in here feet first. Based on the blanching, I'd guess she's been here at least eight hours. I'll get a liver temp when we get her up there, and I have more room to work."

The doctor took more pictures and attempted to straighten the body.

"You need help down there?" Torres asked.

"Yes, but there's not room for anyone else. Let's get her up."

"How should we do that?"

"I don't know. I don't want to be too rough on her and cause any postmortem injuries."

"We could use the planter," Clark said.

"The what?" Torres asked.

"I call it the planter. It's what I use to lower the casket into the vault. We could bring her up on that, provided you got something to lay her on."

"Would a backboard do?" the doctor asked.
Clark rubbed his chin, then spat on his boot. "I reckon that will do just fine."

"There's one in my car."

Torres had an officer retrieve the backboard from the doctor's car and lowered it into the grave. While Seer got the victim ready, Clark went to work setting up his planter.

Clark had a metal frame that he positioned around the grave that consisted of four poles that connected to braces at the corners. One of the long poles that made up the side had two green mesh straps connected to it.

"You all set down there?" Clark asked.

"Yep. She's ready."

"Okay. Look out below. I'll send down the straps, and you put them under the board, then pass them back up to me."

Without waiting for the okay, Clark dropped the two straps into the hole, then watched as the doctor maneuvered them under the body board. He passed each one up, and Clark attached them to the other side pole. When everything was ready, the doctor climbed out of the hole and removed the ladder.

"Okay, here we go," Clark said.

From his pocket, he produced a handle and inserted it into one of the corner supports. He turned the crank, and the side rotated, pulling the straps upward. Clark worked slowly and steady, and after five minutes, the body appeared at ground level.

Two officers appeared at the two ends of the body board and removed the victim from the straps, carried her a few feet away, and set her on the ground. While Dr. Seer moved over to further examine the body, Torres placed the ladder down in the vault and climbed into the hole. She retrieved a flashlight from her belt and turned it on. She shined it throughout the space, looking for any obvious clues, but found nothing. The vault was as clean as the day it made at the factory. Dejected, she left the hole and approached the doctor.

"Find out anything yet?" Torres asked.

"Only cause of death."

"That was quick. Gunshot?"

"Nope."

The doctor opened the victim's mouth a crack and shined his penlight in. Torres could see a shiny piece of red.

"What's that?"

"I'm guessing it's a balloon. She probably choked on it."

"Accident?"

"Doubtful. I'll know more when I do the autopsy. Find anything in the vault?"

Torres shook her head. "Nothing jumped out at me. I sent a tech down for a closer look, but I'd bet there's nothing to find. It's way too clean. When can you get to the autopsy?"

"I was all caught up when I was called out here, so I'll start on her as soon as I get back. Why don't you come visit in a couple of hours and I'll tell you what I found."

Torres nodded and returned to the vault to oversee the

evidence collection.

After an hour of hard work, all the evidence her techs could produce was a single leaf from an oak tree and a small spot of liquid. They'd taken a sample of the liquid, but it took little detecting for Torres to determine it had come from Clark, who spit more than your average llama. She'd gotten a DNA sample from Clark as she took his statement just for comparison's sake.

As for Clark's statement, there wasn't much to go on. The day before, he'd dug the hole and placed the concrete vault in the ground with a backhoe. When he showed up the next morning, he set up the canopy and lined up the chairs. Then he went to work preparing the grave site and noticed the body only when he was putting the fake grass around the area.

Clark's statement and the lack of evidence gave her a whole lot of nothing to go on. The detective was in a surly mood on the ride back to the station, and it had not improved three hours later when she headed into the medical examiner's labyrinth in the basement and found the good Dr. Seer wasn't at his post.

Torres made herself comfortable behind his desk and picked up a magazine and paged through it while she waited. After fifteen minutes, he appeared carrying a white bag that she recognized as being from the deli across the street.

"What do you have there?" Torres asked.

"Nothing special. Ham and cheese on whole wheat. Lettuce, pickles, onions, mayo."

"Get a spear?"

"Of course."

The doctor pulled a chair up to the front of his desk, opened the bag, and unrolled the sub sandwich. Without asking, he took half and gave it to Torres, then rooted around in the bag and found the plastic baggie holding the juicy dill pickle spear and passed that to her as well.

"You have a knife to cut this in half?" Torres asked.

"No. Eat your half and give it back."

"Oh really? What will the new Mrs. Doctor say about that?" Torres teased.

Seer shrugged as he picked up his sandwich. "Probably nothing. We're sharing a pickle, Gloria, not having a baby together."

Torres laughed, then took the pickle from the package and bit into it. It was crunchy, a bit sour, and delicious, just the way pickles should be.

"How did the autopsy go?" she said after she'd finished her half of the pickle.

"Easiest autopsy ever. All of her internal organs appeared normal. No cuts or contusions anywhere. Only injury of note was she had two broken ankles, but I suspect that happened postmortem when she fell into the grave."

"So, the cause of death?"

"Asphyxiation. Someone shoved a balloon in her mouth and inflated it until she choked on it."

"Any chance it was an accident?" Torres asked.

"No way. She had tape residue on both wrists. I'm pretty sure she got held down when this happened."

"I guessing you didn't find any ID on her."

"You'd be right. She's an unknown for now. I sent all her clothing upstairs for analysis. All the lab work from the blood and tissue samples will be back in a few weeks, but it would really surprise me if anything showed up on them. By all appearance's sake, she looked like your average brown-haired, brown-eyed college girl who lived life on the slow side."

"So, in other words, you have absolutely nothing for me."

"Oh, I wouldn't say that. I have a message for you."

The doctor set his sandwich down, lifted the butcher paper, and grabbed a file folder from his desk. From within, he extracted a photograph and passed it to Torres.

"What's this?"

"When I extracted the balloon from her throat, I saw what

looked like writing on it. At first, I thought it might have been one of those promotional balloons like you'd find at a car dealership or carnival. So, I blew up the balloon to see what the writing said."

Torres held up the picture. In it, the balloon looked fully expanded, and the writing on it was clearly readable. "A. I'm coming for you. A? The girl's initial? Like Ashley or Amy?"

Dr. Seer shrugged. "I don't know. That's up for you to figure out, Detective."

CHAPTER SEVEN

Olivia felt the bed shift as Heather woke and turned off the alarm on her phone. She closed her eyes and listened intently as Heather passed through her morning routine. The shower came on and exactly seven minutes later it turned off. Then, after a few minutes, she heard the bathroom sink water turn on as Heather brushed her teeth. The water turned off and Heather came into the bedroom. She toweled off, got into some work clothes, and sat on the bed next to Olivia.

"Liv? Are you awake?"

"Eh?" Olivia said. She feigned a grogginess in her voice.

"I'm headed to work. Are you going to be okay today?"

"Yeah."

"Are you going to get out today, maybe take a walk around the block like Dr. Longstreet suggested?"

"Maybe."

"Do you need anything? Groceries or whatnot?"

"No."

"Okay. I'll call later. I might be able to come back for lunch."

Olivia didn't answer.

"Olivia?"

A moment later, Olivia emitted a light snore, so Heather kissed her on the forehead, covered her with the blanket, and quietly left the apartment.

As soon as Olivia heard the locks rattle into place, Olivia threw back the covers and walked into the living room. She sat off to the edge of the plate-glass window, obscured by the drapes. There, she waited like a cat watching birds in a feeder. A couple of minutes later, Heather left her building and jaywalked across the street, where she got into her car and drove off to start her day. Olivia waited a few minutes to see if Heather might return, but she didn't.

Olivia rushed to the fridge and threw open the freezer door. From way in the back, underneath a half dozen bags of frozen vegetables, Olivia pulled out an ice cube tray. She closed the door, put the tray on the counter, hesitated a second, then retrieved a second one. From the top of the fridge, she brought down the pitcher she used for lemonade. The ice cube trays both had plastic covers on them, so Olivia carefully uncovered them one at a time and dumped the contents into the pitcher. She knew putting vodka in the ice cube tray wouldn't stand up to close scrutiny, especially since the cubes never froze solid. But who ever checked unless they needed ice? From the drying rack next to the sink, she grabbed a glass and filled it with the vodka from the pitcher. She drank half the glass, then filled it again.

After she took another drink, she put down her glass and opened the fridge again. From inside, she grabbed a plastic bowl full of fruits and vegetables that Heather had cut up the night before. She took it over to Nibbler's cage, sampling a couple of pieces of fruit as she went. There was an empty food dish in the cage and Olivia removed it and replaced it with the full one.

"Nibbler. It's breakfast time. You in there?"

Olivia bent down and looked in the mouse house. Nibbler lay in the back of the enclosure, nose on his front paws, tail wrapped around his body. Liv tapped on the cage and Nibbler woke with a squeak.

"Hey, little man, it's time to eat."

Olivia took a raspberry from the bowl and held it right in front of the mouse house entrance. Nibbler squeaked again, then slowly got to his feet and walked toward the treat. He sniffed at the berry a few times, then began to nibble on it. Olivia held on as long as she could, but as Nibbler ate out the berry's center, it collapsed between her fingers. As she withdrew her hand, Nibbler pulled the remaining berry bits between his tiny paws and continued his meal.

Olivia watched the mouse for a moment, wiped the raspberry juice on her pajama bottoms, and returned to her vodka. She drank down half the glass and refilled it from the pitcher. She frowned when she noticed that besides the full glass, there was only an inch of liquid left in the pitcher.

"Damn," she said.

She opened the freezer and checked for an ice tray she may have missed, but found nothing except frozen vegetables, frozen pizza, and frozen waffles. Next, she expanded her search to other areas of the kitchen. The cabinets in the back corners, in the industrial-sized stock pots she used for soups back when she cooked, and in the drawer that held nothing but kitchen towels. She found nothing.

Olivia moved into the living room. She checked inside the window sash, behind the television set, and under the couch. After the living room, she returned to the kitchen and downed another half-glass, then emptied the pitcher. She became methodical and searched her bedroom, bathroom, and every closet. Olivia couldn't find a spare bottle of booze in any of her regular hiding spaces.

"Damn," she said again as she returned to the kitchen. She

sat down on the stool and nursed her glass. Instead of gulping down the last of her alcohol in short order, she forced herself to show some sort of restraint. Five minutes later, the glass stood empty, and Olivia swore at it again.

"Well, glass, I guess we need to go out after all."

Olivia headed toward the bathroom. She thought about a shower, then lifted her arm, sniffed, and decided she'd be okay for the quick trip she had planned. Instead, she ran a brush through her hair and scrubbed her teeth.

In the bedroom, she slipped out of her pajamas, selected a clean pair of panties, and put those on. Rather than decide on the rest of her outfit, she put on the same socks, shirt, sweatshirt, and pants she'd worn the day before.

From the top of her dresser, she grabbed her phone and keys and shoved them both in her pockets. Once she'd put on a pair of sneakers, she appeared ready to go.

Olivia headed to the front door, looked in the peephole, then, seeing no one waiting for her in the hallway, unlocked the locks. She held her hand on the doorknob for almost a minute before she turned it, took a step outside, and closed the door behind her.

In the morning, it typically took Heather no more than four minutes to walk down the stairs and leave the building. It took Olivia three times as long to make the same trip. She paused as she passed each apartment on her floor and stopped on every stair landing. Statue still, she'd listen and wait for someone to appear and snatch her. No one did.

Once she stepped out of the building, she stood on the top step for several minutes, watching the traffic and pedestrians pass by, and listening to the sounds of the city.

"Excuse me."

If Olivia overheard the voice behind her, she didn't acknowledge it.

Olivia jumped and screamed when she felt a hand on her

shoulder. She tripped down the remaining three stairs and landed flat on her butt.

"I'm so sorry," the young Hispanic woman said, who bounded down the stairs and helped Olivia to her feet. "I thought you heard me. You were blocking the way."

Olivia didn't speak.

"Do you live in the building?" the woman asked.

Olivia nodded.

"I'm Maria. I just moved in a few days ago. Are you all right?"

Olivia nodded again. "I'll be fine. I'm sorry I got in your way."

Rather than wait around for more conversation, Olivia gave Maria half a wave, then took off down the block. As she walked, she noticed all kinds of people coming toward her. Moms pushing strollers, men and women with dogs on leashes, joggers, walkers, and one delivery person who stopped at practically every building on the block. As each person got near, Olivia stepped off the sidewalk, giving them plenty of room to pass. In each instance, she got a strange look from the person moving by her.

When she reached the end of the block, Olivia pressed the button to activate the pedestrian light, then stepped back from the street. When the little green walk signal lit up, Olivia ran across the street, not wanting to spend any more time in the street than she needed to.

Halfway up the block she came to a small bodega and entered the shop. She snaked through the aisles, not finding what she was searching for, so she stopped at the front counter.

"Do you have any vodka?" she asked the clerk.

The clerk turned around and searched for his liquor supply. "Vodka? I've only got a quarter pint." The clerk held it up.

It wasn't a brand Olivia recognized, and it was a smaller

bottle than she wanted, but she whipped out her debit card and bought it, anyway. The clerk wrapped it in a brown paper bag, and Olivia left the store. When she got to the corner of the building, she slipped into a side alley, removed the bottle from the bag, and opened it. Since it held only twice the amount of the travel-sized bottles, she emptied it in only a few gulps, put the bottle back in the bag, and dropped it next to the building.

Olivia headed back to the sidewalk. Before moving on, she looked to her left and right. To the left was the nearest grocery store, which she knew held an impressive liquor section. To the right was home with water and lemonade. As she looked to the right, she spotted someone halfway up the block on the other side of the street. She thought it was a man, wearing all black. Black shoes, black jeans, and a black sweatshirt with the hood up over his head.

Olivia turned left and speed-walked up the sidewalk. She crossed a street and when she got a few feet away from the corner, she stopped and looked behind her.

The man in black was still there. Still on the opposite side of the street, still about the same amount of distance away. She took a few more steps, then turned around. The man had moved as well, but was now standing still, just like Olivia.

She spun and moved at a slow jog, no longer trying to avoid people. Several she passed with room to spare, and a couple she ran into but kept going. After a hundred yards, she turned around and looked. The man was right where she expected him to be.

Since Olivia was only a hundred yards away from the safety of the store, she broke into a run and sprinted as fast as she could to the entrance and slowed only after she got through the door. She stepped outside looking for the man, but the store's angle and the cars in the parking lot prevented her from seeing anyone.

Olivia entered the store, grabbed a red plastic basket, and

headed right for the liquor aisle. She stopped before the precious vodka. She loaded the basket with four double-magnum sized bottles but had trouble lifting it. Olivia removed the bottles from the basket and filled the basket with liters instead. She had extra room in there and was about to fill in the empty space when the man in black passed through her peripheral vision.

Shocked, she stood and backed up until she came in contact with the shelf behind her with enough force to knock several bottles of Australian red wine from the shelves. They fell, exploding like tiny bombs as they hit the floor, covering the area in varying shades of red. Olivia slid down the shelf and sat on the floor, noticing neither her wet pants nor the shards of glass cutting into her flesh.

* * *

Heather waited in the chair in front of Detective Torres's desk. She didn't enjoy being there and developed a nervous tic from her anxiety that caused her leg to shake up and down. Heather checked her phone again and saw she'd been sitting in the chair for thirty-five minutes, and it had been almost ninety minutes since she'd received the call. She thought about getting up and walking around a bit to dissipate her energy, but the first time she did that, the first police officer that spotted her escorted her right back to the chair.

She checked the clock. Another minute passed. At last, Heather picked up familiar voices from the hallway, and a moment later, the detective's door opened and Torres escorted Olivia into the room.

"Sit there," the detective said, pointing to the chair next to Heather.

Olivia did so without speaking. She felt Heather's gaze upon her and responded by staring at the floor.

"What happened?" Heather asked.

"Well, funny story. Your friend here got drunk, entered a grocery store, and knocked over a dozen bottles of wine." Detective Torres said.

"There was someone chasing me," Olivia muttered, not looking up.

Heather looked from Olivia to Torres. "Is that true?"

"She seems to think it is. The officers took her statement at the scene. Neither witnesses nor the in-store security feed could confirm her story."

Olivia lifted her head. "There was a man. In black. All black. He followed me. I saw him. I'm not crazy!"

Heather looked at her friend. Olivia's eyes were red, as if she'd been crying for an hour. Her hair and clothes looked disheveled. She wore a pair of bright orange jail pants.

"What's up with the pants?" Heather asked.

"Wine," Detective Torres said. "You can pick them up at the desk on your way out. Look. I know all about what she suffered through, and I know it's affected her. You're both lucky that the booking sergeant contacted me when they brought her in. I've talked to the store, and they've agreed to drop the charges provided Olivia pays for all the merchandise she damaged. They've also banned her from there for a year. I'm also dropping the public intoxication charges."

"So, she's free to go?"

"For now. But if this happens again, I might have to hold her. Take her home. Pump her full of coffee and sober her up. Keep her out of trouble."

"Okay, Detective. I'll try. Let's get out of here, Olivia. Thank you for everything."

Heather stood and took Olivia's elbow and guided her to her feet. Together, they left the office and stopped at the desk to pick up Olivia's personal items. As Olivia waited for her possessions, Heather stepped off to the side of the room and called the doctor.

"Come on, you've got an appointment," Heather said once Olivia had her things together.

"Do we have to? I have a splitting headache. I want to go home and go to bed."

"No. We're going to see the doctor."

Heather led Olivia out of the station and got her situated in the car. Once she got in the driver's seat and started the engine, she sniffed the air.

"What's that smell?"

Olivia held up the plastic bag holding her pants. "Probably this. I guess I spilled some wine."

Heather grabbed the bag from Olivia, got out of the car, and went to the trunk. There, she found a stray plastic bag, wrapped Olivia's bag in the new one, and tied it shut. She left the whole mess in the trunk and got back in her seat.

"Can I at least go home and change pants?"

"Nope. Sorry. The doctor's waiting for us."

Olivia shrank in her seat as Heather put the car in gear and sped away from the curb. Ten minutes later, she arrived in front of Dr. Longstreet's building. Heather parked the car, but Olivia made no attempt to get out. Heather let out a loud sigh and stepped around to Olivia's door, opened it, and physically pulled Olivia from the SUV. Once outside, Olivia capitulated and went quietly up the stairs and into the building.

The receptionist wasn't there, but Dr. Longstreet was waiting in the outer office.

"Would you join us for this one, Heather?"

The doctor led the women into the inner office. Heather and Olivia took the chairs in front of the desk, and the doctor took the seat behind it.

"Who wants to tell me what happened?" Dr. Longstreet asked.

Heather and Olivia looked at each other for an extended

time.

"Olivia, this is your story," Heather said. "Tell her everything, just like you remembered it."

"I can try. Some of it is pretty foggy, though," she said.

"That's fine," Dr. Longstreet said. "Tell me what you do remember. We can work through the rest together if we need to."

Olivia nodded, then started recounting the story. Occasionally, the doctor would stop and ask a clarifying question, but other than that, she let Olivia tell the tale. Heather stayed silent the entire time, not asking any questions or making any statements. After forty minutes, Olivia finished.

"Olivia, could you go wait outside while I talk to Heather for a minute?" the doctor asked.

Olivia didn't object. She simply stood and walked out of the room.

"You mentioned on the phone earlier that she was drunk?" the doctor asked.

"Yes. From what I understand, she was that way before she even entered the store."

"She didn't mention any alcohol when she told us what happened just now."

"I noticed. I think she's in denial. Is she drinking? Without a doubt, I know she's been drinking, but I don't know where she's getting it. I check her favorite hiding spots every day."

"How much do you think she's drinking?"

"That I can't tell you. I suspect it's quite a bit, but I can't prove it," Heather said. "Do you have any suggestions?"

"A couple, actually. The first is to get her into a program. I can help her process the trauma she's been through, but if she's masking it with alcohol, that's going to make my work almost impossible. There's a high probability that we're discussing things in here that she doesn't even remember. It's useless for me to give her coping techniques if she doesn't remember to follow through with them."

"Makes sense," Heather said. "What's the other?"

"Normally I wouldn't suggest this because of privacy issues, but in this case, you might install a couple of cameras in her apartment. Not in the bedroom or bathroom, of course, but in the common areas. That may help you determine how much she's drinking and where she's getting it from."

Heather thought about it for a moment. "I'd prefer not to do that."

"I agree. But if things get worse with her, you might not have a choice."

CHAPTER EIGHT

Detective Torres arrived at the fishing dock at three minutes after eleven.

"What do we have, Jansen?"

"Two fishermen found a body in the river about a half mile downstream from here."

"What can you tell me about it?" Torres asked.

"Actually, nothing. I'm only here to secure the dock. The boat should be back in a moment to get you. It just ran the doctor down to the site."

"Who got the call?"

"Dr. Seer. He didn't seem overly happy about getting called out here."

"I'm sure he's got a good reason for it," Torres said.

The two stood in silence and waited. After a few more minutes, a drone of a boat engine headed toward the dock. When it got close, the boat driver pulled alongside and tossed the stern and bow lines to Jansen. He held them tight until Torres got on the boat and tossed them back to the captain. Torres took a seat as the boat pulled away from the dock and kept her eye on the river as the boat headed downstream.

Torres spotted the crime scene long before they arrived. It was on the far side of the river, at a spot where the river bent inward to the shore and created a cove about twenty feet long. She saw several people on the scene, including three of her officers and the doctor. Two fishermen sat on the bank nearby, dressed in matching rubber hip waders. Torres thought they might be brothers, but as the boat crept closer, she decided they were most likely father and son.

"I'm going to let you off up ahead. You'll have to walk the rest of the way in," the boat captain announced.

Without waiting for a response, the captain steered the boat toward the shore and cut the throttle and let it drift toward the bank. He stood at the bow and a moment before the boat hit the land; he jumped to shore, pulled on the bowline, and swung the boat around.

"All ashore who's going ashore," the captain said, and Torres easily stepped from the boat to the bank.

From there, the detective found a deer trail and followed it to within a few yards of the scene, then cut through the trees and ended up at the cove where she found Dr. Seer bent over a body.

"Hey, Jimmy," Torres said as she approached.

"Gloria."

"I'm surprised to see you out here."

The doctor stood and turned around. He looked out over the river, then at the detective. "I am too. I was lucky enough to be next in the rotation, so here I am."

"Still not a fan of water?" she asked.

"Not since that day," he said.

The day in question happened when the detective and the doctor were only Glory and Jimmy, and the pair were both thirteen. Glory got the idea of making a fort in the woods, but to do it, they needed to cross a stream. Rather than use a perfectly good bridge a hundred yards upstream, Glory wanted to cross using a downed tree. She crossed without incident. Jimmy, on the other hand, got his foot caught on a branch, did a somersault off the tree, and landed headfirst in the stream. The impact was enough to knock him out cold for a few seconds, and when he came to, he found himself under water. He panicked, inhaled, and took in a lungful of river, which caused even more panic. He couldn't tell which way was up, couldn't get his feet underneath him.

"I'm sorry about what happened," Torres said.

"What happened was we were kids doing stupid kid stuff. I got into trouble, and you saved me."

"That's not the way I remember it," Torres said.

"I believe your memory is off. Because I remember I was about to die, and you jumped into that creek and pulled me out. Then you punched me in the stomach until I threw up all that water. Hardly an approved Red Cross method for first aid."

Torres shrugged. "What did I understand about rescue back in the dark ages? I wanted to be a horse vet, not a lifesaver. So, what do we have here? A drowning?"

"I'm not a hundred percent sure. I just got here myself. Based on what I see, I don't believe she was in the river. I'm pretty sure she got dumped here."

"What makes you think that?"

"I've seen river drownings before. Usually, the body gets beat up from being dragged by the current. They end up with lots of cuts and contusions on the body, and there's usually detritus such as leaves, sticks, and river plants on them. She seems to have none of those."

"Why dump her here?"

"Ask them," Seer said, pointing toward the two fishermen.

"I think I will. I'll be right back."

Torres made her way to the anglers. As she got close, one of her officers saw her coming and handed her both men's driver's licenses. She glanced at them and based on the last name, their common address, and dates of birth, she concluded she'd been right about the father and son relationship.

"I have a couple of questions, fellas. What time did you get here?"

"About three hours ago. When we spotted her, we called the police right away."

"Did you touch the body?"

He shook his head. "Nope. Seen enough television cop shows to know better than to do that. Seen all kinds of things come into that cove, but never expected to see anything like that. I don't think my boy will ever get over it."

"You've been to the cove before?" Torres asked.

"Of course. Every sportsman on the river knows about this cove. It's one of the best places to fish. It makes for a natural cover for them and it's always a guaranteed catch."

"Do other people fish there?"

"Oh, for sure. Actually, it surprised me to have it to ourselves this morning. Like I said, it's one of the most popular spots around."

The detective handed the dad both licenses. "Thanks, fellas. You can go."

She returned to the doctor, who was busy examining the body. "According to those men, this is a popular fishing spot and there's always people here."

"So, someone dumped her in this location, knowing someone would find her in no time?"

"That's what I'm thinking. Do you know how she died?"

"I only now figured it out," the doctor said. "Can you hand me an evidence bag and a forceps from my backpack?"

Torres retrieved the requested items. She held the bag and handed over the forceps to the doctor. He took it, opened the woman's mouth, and used it to remove an item from her throat.

"That's not what I think it is," Torres said.

Dr. Seer dropped it into the evidence bag. "A red balloon."

Torres sealed the bag, then turned it over. "There's writing on it."

"I'm not surprised. Can you read it?"

Torres stretched out the balloon as much as she could. "It says I'm coming for you. And there's a capital letter I."

"Sounds like bad news," the doctor said.

"Yeah. Sounds like we have a serial. Damn."

* * *

Olivia, remote in hand, stared at the television for twelve minutes straight.

"Do you plan on watching something?" Daphne asked. "I may only be a figment of your imagination, but even I know all you need to do is push that little red button at the top and the set will magically turn on."

Olivia glanced next to her and waved the remote at the vision. "Well, hello. I haven't seen you in a long time. Where have you been?"

Her old science teacher shrugged. "Here and there, visiting the cosmos. What's new with you?"

"Nothing," Olivia answered.

"You've got a problem. You need to work it out."

"How do you know that?" Olivia looked at the woman. When she'd seen her months before, she appeared just as Olivia had remembered her in school. Jeans, button-down shirt, long hair pinned back, reading glasses dangling in the center of her shirt with one arm tucked over the collar. Now Daphne Blake looked completely different. She was bright and shimmering, and had no colors, yet all colors at once. Her voice remained as Olivia had remembered it, questioning yet gentle.

"Because you always call me when you need me the most."

"But I don't need you. I don't need anyone!" Olivia shouted. For dramatic effect, she threw the remote on the floor. The plastic case broke in two and the batteries popped out.

"That's never going to work now," Daphne said. "But you shouldn't concern yourself with such things. You have a problem. You have to work the problem."

"The only problem I have is that you people won't leave me alone!"

Olivia sprung from the couch and wandered into the kitchen. She opened the freezer looking for more of her secret vodka-filled ice cube trays but couldn't find any. Exasperated, she dug deeper through the frozen food, dropping bags of frozen vegetables on the floor as she did. Not finding what she wanted, Olivia walked away from the fridge without closing the door. She moved on to the bathroom, stopped at the toilet, and lifted the lid from the tank.

"What are you looking for?" Daphne asked.

"You already know what I'm looking for." Olivia looked down and spotted nothing but the inner workings of the toilet tank. She replaced the lid but left it askew.

Next, she wandered into the bedroom. She bypassed the closet and all the furniture and headed to the window, unlocked it, and pushed up the pane. Outside the window a small wrought-iron decorative feature held a plastic flower box the color of brick. When she moved in, Olivia lined the box with a patch of fake grass and added four clay flowerpots filled with fake daisies. She leaned out the window and reached for the corner closest to the building and farthest to her left. Olivia moved the flowerpot and peeled back the fake grass.

"Eureka!" she yelled as she pulled a pint of vodka from the box. She tossed it on the bed and checked the box, discovering she had three more tucked away in there, like a squirrel stocking up on nuts for the winter. Once she replaced the grass and the flowerpot, she closed the window, picked up the vodka, and returned to the living room.

Olivia opened the bottle, took a long swig, and placed the

bottle on the table next to her. She retrieved the pieces of the remote and snapped everything back together. She pointed it at the television, pushed the red button, and nothing happened.

"You've got the batteries in backward," Daphne said.

"Do not," Olivia said. She pushed the button again, and when nothing happened, she opened the remote, turned around the batteries, and tried again.

The television sprang to life and Olivia flipped through the channels at lightning speed until she landed on one and stopped. She turned the volume down low and grabbed the bottle.

"Cartoons?" Daphne asked. "You couldn't find something more educational, like a science program, or perhaps one of those shows where the host tries to determine who the baby's daddy is?"

Olivia shrugged. "I like the colors. Besides, these are classic cartoons, not like the crap of today. What difference is it to you, anyway? You're imaginary."

Daphne turned her attention to the television and watched a coyote run full speed into the side of a mountain. "Okay, you win. At least it's the classics. Now, Olivia, what are you going to do about your problem? You need to work it."

Olivia picked up her bottom. "Wrong. The only thing I need to work on is this. Watch this."

She inverted the bottle and drained three-quarters of the contents at once. After it was empty, she let it drop to the floor and wiped her mouth with the sleeve of her pajama top.

"How's that for working the stupid problem?" Olivia shouted.

As she waited for Daphne to respond, Olivia felt her stomach roll. Then a large gurgle came boiling up from deep inside her.

"Ah, crap," she said as she pushed herself off the couch.

Olivia ran to the kitchen, her stomach protesting with every step. Just as she got two feet from the sink, the vomit rose from the depths, and although she tried not to let it go until she reached the sink, it proved too much for her. The returning vodka erupted from Olivia's mouth and sprayed the front of the sink, the floor, half of the island, and the front of her shirt. When she finally reached the sink, she clutched the counter for support, dropped her head into the bowl and let it flow freely. She heaved several times, and when her stomach emptied, she took three deep breaths and turned on the water. She rinsed her mouth several times and grabbed a nearby dish towel and wiped her face.

Slowly, Olivia straightened herself. Her stomach ached and her head pounded. After she blinked hard a few times to clear the spiderwebs in her head, she looked up to assess the damage. She used the towel to wipe the mess from the island top and took a step backward. When she did, Olivia stepped on a bag of frozen peas she'd chucked to the floor earlier. She slipped, almost maintained her balance, then fell, striking her head on the fridge on the way down. Olivia was unconscious before she landed in a puddle of her own regurgitations.

Olivia dreamed and, in her dream, Daphne kept hitting Olivia in the center of the forehead with her finger. Her touch wasn't as warm as inviting as in the old days but was now cold and lifeless.

"Olivia. Get up. Work the problem," Daphne said each time she tapped Olivia.

After the tenth time Daphne poked her in the head, Olivia opened her eyes. She was flat on her back, staring at the kitchen ceiling. Olivia could also see the open freezer door, and a second later she saw a drop of water fall. She watched it all the way down and didn't even attempt to move when it hit her right in the middle of her forehead, directly where Daphne's continuous jabs had hit her.

Olivia groaned and put her hand down to roll over, and it landed in a wet pile. After several moments, her head cleared, and she remembered what had happened to her. She managed to turn over, and when she did, she got blasted by the foul odor of expelled vodka mixed with whatever she'd last eaten. With the help of the island, she climbed to her feet, lurched to the other side of it, and sat on a stool.

She glanced at the time on the microwave, which read all zeros as it usually did, so she turned her attention to the stove's time instead. It read half-past three. She knew that time was usually off by a couple of minutes in either direction, but she also knew that Heather would arrive within the hour.

"Damn. We've got a problem to work out now, Daphne."

Olivia started the cleanup by forcing herself to drink a glass of water, and she went to work. She gathered up all the freezer items she'd dropped to the floor, rinsed them all in the sink, threw them back into the freezer and slammed the door shut. Next, she retrieved the all-purpose cleaner and paper towels from underneath the sink. She sprayed the entire area, including the floor, with the cleaner and wiped it all up with the paper towels. She dumped them all into the kitchen garbage, then retrieved her empty vodka bottle and added that to the trash. Once the kitchen was in order, she left her apartment long enough to drop the garbage down the trash chute.

When she got back to the apartment, Olivia went into the bathroom and stripped out of her pajamas. She made the mistake of smelling the shirt and retched again. She carried her pajamas to the washing machine and dumped them in. Feeling two items of clothing did a load not make, Olivia retrieved her clothes hamper from the bedroom, and tossed additional things into the washer without bothering to sort through them. She closed the washer, turned it on, then took a half-dozen steps toward the bathroom but she returned to the washer and added soap.

Back in the bathroom, Olivia removed the hair tie to release her ponytail and turned on the water in the shower. While she waited for a decent temperature, she brushed her teeth twice. Once completed with that task, she noticed the ajar toilet tank cover and fixed it before stepping in to the shower.

Olivia washed her hair first. After a long shampoo and longer rinse, she brushed the hair and water away from her eyes.

"I'm glad you're in here. When was the last time you took a shower? A week? More?" Daphne said.

"Why are you in my shower?"

"You still have a problem to work," Daphne said.

"Well, I'm certainly not going to do it right now! And certainly not with you in my shower!" Olivia screamed over the pounding water. "Why don't you go haunt someone else?"

Olivia grabbed the bodywash from the shelf and squeezed it in Daphne's direction. Had she actually been there, she would have caught the glop right on her chin.

"Well, I never," Daphne declared, then faded away.

"Olivia?"

"Shut up and go away!" Olivia screamed.

The bathroom door opened, and Heather entered. "Olivia?"

Olivia stuck her head out from behind the curtain. "Oh. It's you. Sorry."

"Who did you think it would be? Are you okay?"

"Yeah. I'm fine."

"I'm going to rummage through the freezer and see what I should make for dinner, okay?"

"Okay."

Heather stepped out and had almost closed the door.

"Heather!" Olivia yelled.

The door opened, and Heather's head appeared. "Yeah?"

"Forget the freezer. Can we order in some Thai tonight?"

Heather hesitated. "Sure. See you when you're done."

CHAPTER NINE

"Would you like a donut?"

Detective Torres looked up from her computer screen and saw Dr. Seer standing before her holding a small white bag in one hand and his laptop in the other.

"You do know that cops and their love of donuts is a long-standing trope. An overused and unfunny one at that," Torres said.

The smile faded from the doctor's face, and he lowered the sack. "But I got a Boston Creme for you."

Torres hesitated for a second. "From Zander's Bakery?"

Seer nodded. "I made the trip downtown. Special. Just for you."

"Okay, Jimmy. Hand over the sack."

"What about the trope concerning cops and donuts?"

Torres smiled. "Just because it's a trope, it doesn't mean it's not true."

She opened the bag, looked inside, and removed the chocolate-topped donut covered in a square of wax paper. "Nothing in here for you?"

"I ate mine on the way in."

Torres flattened the bag and set the donut on top of it. She eyed it for a moment and took a bite. After she swallowed it down with a sip of cold coffee, she smiled. "Thanks. I haven't had one of these in a long time. What's the reason for the visit? It's not my birthday."

"I've got some of the test results back from those two related cases."

"Okay," Torres said. She picked up the donut and continued to work on it while Seer unfolded his laptop and set it on the corner of her desk. "I can show you mine since you're going to show me yours."

Torres took a couple of minutes to finish her donut and drained her coffee. She hit a few buttons on her laptop and turned it around so Seer could see.

"Our victims?" the doctor asked.

"Yep. Ainsley Hall on the left, Isabel Gill on the right."

"They could be twin sisters," Seer said. "I guess the A and I on the notes make sense now."

The two photographs were from the Department of Transportation. The pictures showed each had long brown hair and brown eyes. A quick examination of the data on the licenses told the doctor that they were within an inch tall from each other, the same weight, and born five months apart.

"I suspect the parents of both will contact the morgue within the hour," Torres said.

"I'll make sure they're ready to be released."

Torres nodded. "Good. Now, what do you have for me?"

"As I suspected, the blood and tissue tests came back mostly normal. No drugs in either of their systems except one."

"You've got my attention," Torres said.

"They both registered off the charts with the amount of clonazepam in their systems."

"What's that?"

"It's a long-acting tranquilizer in the benzodiazepine class. Typically, it's prescribed to help people with several disorders, including anxiety, bipolar, and obsessive-compulsive. It's also given to help with seizures."

"Were they on prescriptions for it?"

"That will be up to you to figure out, but I'm guessing not. The dosages were too high. With the amount that was in their system, they would have become sedated and open to hypnotic suggestion."

"So, someone slipped it in a drink? Or food?"

"Nope. Look here." The doctor clicked on a file and opened a photograph. "What you're looking at here is a puncture wound. I found it on the thigh of victim one. I mean Ainsley. Isabel had a similar puncture on her left hip."

"Okay. We have two almost identical women, both drugged identically. Both killed identically. Both dumped in places where their bodies would get discovered in short order," Torres said.

"What's the plan going to be here?" the doctor asked.

The detective opened her mouth to answer, but before she could utter a word, her desk phone rang.

"Hold on," she said to the doctor, then picked up the phone. "Torres." She listened for almost a full minute, then slammed down the phone without saying a word.

"Let's go get your gear, Jimmy. We've got another one."

"You want to ride with me or meet me there?"

"Let's take your wagon," Torres said.

Thirty minutes later, Doctor Seer turned the medical examiner's wagon into Grant Park. The park was the largest in town and contained a soccer field, two baseball diamonds, a basketball court, and four tennis courts, along with several picnic areas and one of the largest children's play areas in the state.

"Whoops," the doctor said as he made a left turn. He brought the vehicle to a stop, then reversed direction until he backed on the road he was on and turned right. "It's been a while since I've been out here."

Convinced he was on the correct road, Seer drove past a splash pad and headed into the depths of the park. Up ahead, they spotted the green roof of a large pavilion, and both saw the flashing lights of the responding officers. Dr. Seer slowed and pulled onto the grass when he got within twenty feet of the structure.

"You ready for this?" Torres asked.

"Not really. Remember how your dad always tried to talk me into becoming a mechanic and working in his shop?"

Torres smiled at the memory. "Yes."

"I should have listened to him."

Seer shut down the ignition and opened the door with Torres following a second behind.

Under the pavilion were six large picnic tables in three rows of two, each made of wood, each six feet in length, each scarred with the graffiti of a hundred bored teenagers. On the back table in the middle row, a woman appeared to be sleeping on the table.

She lay flat on her back, her bare heels together, hands palm down at her side. Underneath her head, a denim jacket acted as a pillow. Beneath the table sat a pair of light blue canvas shoes, and in each was stuffed a neatly folded white sock.

Torres looked around the area. There were four officers on the scene. One was taking the statement of a young mother, one was busy wrapping yellow police line tape around the pavilion supports, one was taking photographs, and one was leaning against his patrol car looking bored.

Dr. Seer put his bag on an adjacent table and from it withdrew his camera and the few tools he knew he'd need. After he snapped on a pair of gloves, he approached the body.

"Look familiar?" he asked Torres.

"Hair and body type match, for sure. What about her eyes?" Torres asked.

Seer leaned over the body and tenderly opened the lids to

check the eye color. "Brown."

"Can you check…" Torres started.

"Give me a minute to follow the procedure," Seer answered.

He grabbed the camera from the table and took pictures of the body from all angles, and once he seemed satisfied he had all the shots he needed, he turned his attention to the woman's mouth. He opened it and shined his penlight into her mouth.

"I'm going to need some help with this one. Can you hold her mouth open for me?" he asked Torres.

Torres donned her own gloves, then stepped up to the table. Seer told her how to position her hands, so she tilted the victim's head back a bit and opened her mouth.

Seer leaned over the body close enough to where his nose almost touched the victim's cheek and shined his light down her throat. He inserted the forceps almost all the way in, closed them, and pulled.

"This got really wedged in there. I think she swallowed part of it."

The doctor added more force to his pull, and the balloon sprung free, making a sickening pop like the release of a wine bottle cork as it did. Torres released the woman's head and gently set it down. She produced an evidence bag, and Dr. Seer dropped the balloon into it.

"You want to do the honors?" Seer asked.

"Not really. I've seen this movie twice too many times already, but it's the job I need to do."

Torres manipulated the balloon until she could read the writing. "This one has a letter V. Same message, though. I'm coming for you."

"I'm going to make a wild guess and say the toxicology report is going to come out the same on her as it did the others."

"Hopefully we'll be able to identify her a little quicker," Torres said.

Torres turned and placed the evidence bag on the table with

the doctor's things, and when she turned back, she inadvertently kicked the pair of shoes under the table.

"Damn," she said.

"Messing up the evidence?" Seer asked. "The captain won't like that."

"Corporal, can you round me up a large evidence bag?" Torres called out to the one officer not doing anything.

Torres bent over, picked up the shoes, and placed them on the table.

"There's something in this one," she said as she lifted the right shoe.

While Seer took photos, Torres removed the sock from the sneaker. She shook it out, found nothing, and placed it on the table. When she looked into the shoe, she spotted a phone. Carefully, she removed it and pressed the button on the side. It lit up.

"It's locked," Torres said, showing Seer the phone.

"That's easy enough to fix. Lay the phone flat."

Torres held the phone while the doctor gently lifted the woman's arm, extended her index finger, and pressed it against the phone screen. A moment later, the phone unlocked.

"Before you go digging around in there, turn the security off," Seer said.

Torres passed him a look of irritation. "This isn't my first case, you know, Doctor."

After Torres unlocked the phone for good, she rooted around for information. "Virginia Parks is her name."

"V for Virginia," Seer said. "Any indication of her last whereabouts? One of those track your family apps, or something on the calendar, or a phone call, or anything?"

"I've got her mother's number in here, and… this is interesting."

"What?" Seer asked.

"I know someone in her text messages."

Torres turned the phone around. Although Dr. Seer didn't recognize the name in the chat history, Torres sure did. Olivia Branch.

* * *

Olivia sat on the couch, her knees up to her chest, her arms wrapped around them, trying to control the shakes.

"I'm so hot," she said. "It must be a hundred degrees in here."

Olivia jumped up and threw open the windows of the living room, then stepped over to the thermostat and pushed the down button on the temperature setting several times. Regardless of how many times or how hard she jabbed it, it wouldn't drop below sixty-six.

"Damn thing," she said.

Olivia made her way back to the window and glanced outside. The leaves on the trees lining the street seemed to accept that winter was on the way and had begun to convert the green leaves to browns and oranges. She watched as a couple passed below her window, each person wearing a heavy sweatshirt and gloves.

"So, hot," Olivia said. She stepped into the kitchen, turned on the cold-water tap, and splashed her face. In doing so, so got the front of her T-shirt all wet, so she stripped it off and let it drop to the floor, leaving her bare chested.

"It's not hot, Olivia," Daphne said. "It's you. You need to work this problem. It's already getting out of hand."

"Why do you keep bothering me?" Olivia asked. She lifted the sprayer from the sink and sent a stream of water in Daphne's direction, wetting the island and the floor beyond in the process.

"A little water won't get me to go away. I'm not a witch. All that will do is irritate you."

Olivia huffed and shut off the water. She stormed from

around the island, headed for the front window. On the way, she stepped into the puddle she'd just created.

"Ugh. I hate wet socks," Olivia said. She sat down on the couch and peeled off one sock, then tossed it across the room. It landed on a shelf and dangled there, as if waiting to be filled on Christmas eve.

"You need help, Olivia," Daphne said.

Olivia went to the window and leaned out into the cool autumn air. A breeze came through and licked at the beads of water on Olivia's face and in her hair. She sighed and closed her eyes, letting the cold wash over her.

"Nice show, babe!" a voice yelled from below.

Olivia opened her eyes and looked at the street. Beneath her window, she spotted a couple of men wearing football jerseys from the local college.

"Eff off," Olivia said. She gave them a one-finger wave, then backed away from the window and closed the curtains. "Jerks."

"Can't hardly blame them. It's not every day you see a half-naked woman dangling from a window," Daphne said.

"You're not helping."

Olivia did a manic circle around the living room, then headed to the bedroom window box and returned a minute later with a fifth of vodka from her secret stash. She collapsed onto the couch, broke the seal on the bottle, and took a drink.

"Heather will be here soon," Daphne warned. "You don't want her to see you like this, do you?"

Olivia drank again, then waved her hand in the air. "Bah. Heather. I'm getting sick of Heather. Why does she think she needs to come over all the time? She's not my mother. I'm perfectly capable of taking care of myself."

Olivia took another two swigs. A bit of liquid dribbled from her chin. She wanted to wipe it with her shirt, but realized she wasn't wearing one, and used a throw pillow instead.

"You're far from capable," Daphne said. "You still sleep with the lights on and wake up screaming half the time. And all the drinking. Olivia. You have a problem. Work it."

"God, Daphne, you're such a pill. I don't have a problem. I swear, you're worse than Heather sometimes with all the constant fussing."

"Olivia. It's not me. It's literally you."

"Bah," Olivia said. She drank again, then looked at the bottle. She'd already drained half of it. "I have more important problems. I only have two of these little beauties left in stock. Oh, man. I really should look around and see if I have some anywhere else. I think Heather found them all, though. Ugh. Heather."

Olivia took another drink and looked at the bottle. Since there wasn't a lot of liquid left, she emptied the bottle, settled into the couch, and closed her eyes.

Olivia opened her eyes when she heard a key rattle in the lock. At first, she didn't recognize where she was, and then it came to her. She looked down, saw the empty bottle in her hand, and panicked. Realizing she had no decent place to put it, she dropped it through the gap between the wall and the back of the couch.

The last lock released, and Heather entered the room, her arms burdened with grocery bags.

"Why is it so cold in here?" she asked herself. As she passed the thermometer, she checked the reading. "Sixty-six? Olivia? Are you here?"

Heather went to the kitchen, moved to put her bags down, and noticed the standing water. Instead of the island, she placed the bags on the stovetop, grabbed a towel, and wiped up the water. Afterward, she picked up the shirt lying on the floor. The curtain fluttered, catching Heather's attention, and when she looked into the living room, she spotted Olivia on the couch.

"Hey there. What are you doing?"

Olivia straightened to a sitting position. "Uh, I was doing some things around the house and sat down for a minute to rest."

"Understandable. But why are you doing it half naked and with one sock on?" Heather asked.

Olivia shrugged.

Heather approached the couch and sat down, then leaned over and brought Olivia in for a hug. "It's okay. Everything will be okay. Where's your other sock? Did you put it on this morning?"

Olivia pointed across the room at the sock that Santa hadn't yet filled.

Heather got up and retrieved the sock. "Gross. It's all wet. Stay there. I'll be right back."

Olivia sat still as instructed, and Heather returned in a few minutes. She'd changed out of her work clothes and into sweatpants and a lavender-colored T-shirt.

"Here, put this on," she said as she handed Olivia a fresh shirt. "Is your other sock wet, too?"

Olivia lifted her leg, and Heather ran her hand along the bottom of her foot. "Yep."

Heather removed the sock from Olivia's foot and replaced it with a green one with yellow stripes, then had Olivia hold up her other foot and added a yellow sock with green stripes to that one.

"Better?"

Olivia nodded.

Heather sat back and wrapped her arm around her friend.

"Did you talk to anyone today?"

"No."

"Your parents didn't call? Or any of the girls?"

"Gabby did," Olivia said.

"Oh, great. Did you have a pleasant talk?"

"We didn't talk. She called while I was in the shower," Olivia lied. In reality, she'd been sitting on the couch eating whipped cream directly from the can when she saw the call come in. She returned to the business of getting another mouthful of creamy goodness and let the call pass to voice mail.

"Talk to Dr. Longstreet today?"

"No. I have an appointment in a couple of days. I got mad at you today."

"Oh yeah, what for?" Heather asked.

"You know, I don't really remember."

"Are you still mad at me?"

Olivia put her hand on Heather's thigh. "No. I'm sorry."

"There's nothing to be sorry for. Do you want to help me make dinner? We're having spaghetti."

Olivia smiled. "That's one of my favorites. I can help."

"Great. Let's get at it then."

Heather waited while Olivia rose and padded into the kitchen. As she pushed on the couch to boost herself up, she felt something between the cushions. She pulled the item free and examined it. A cap from a vodka bottle. Heather shook her head, put the cap in her pocket, and headed for the kitchen.

CHAPTER TEN

Olivia woke to a pounding at her door that matched the pounding in her head. She opened her eyes, rolled over, grabbed her phone, and checked the time. It was a few minutes before ten. The green box told her she'd missed a half-dozen calls, and when she investigated, she determined they had all come in from the same unlisted number.

The noise from the front door repeated, and Olivia wondered if Heather had lost her key since a random stranger wouldn't be able to make it through the locked building entrance.

"I'm coming," Olivia said, not much louder than a whisper.

When she threw back the comforter, Olivia discovered she was naked, which wasn't a complete surprise. Six nights out of the last seven, she'd overheated in her pajamas and stripped them off in the middle of the night. Now, throwing her feet over the side, she shivered and realized she'd not only gotten down to her birthday suit, but had also thrown the window wide open. The rapping at the door came again, this time deeper in tone.

Half asleep and naked, Olivia plodded into the living room and stood next to the door.

"Who's there?" she yelled and immediately regretted it. She placed her palms against her temples to fight off the headache.

"Olivia Branch?" said the response.

"Who are you?" Olivia said, while considering returning to bed.

"It's Detective Gloria Torres from the police department."

"Bull." Olivia stretched onto her tippy toes and looked through the peephole in the door. There stood a woman who looked familiar, but Olivia couldn't remember why. She didn't dress like a cop, though. "Can you show me some ID?"

Torres sighed and dug her credentials from the inside pocket of her coat, opened them, and held them up to the peephole. "Come on, Olivia. We've already met. Can you let me in? There's a matter we need to discuss."

"I'm not dressed. Can you wait a minute?" Olivia said.

"I'll be here," Torres said.

Olivia padded into the kitchen and poured a glass of water from the faucet. The cabinet next to the fridge held not only the glasses but also a large bottle of acetaminophen that Heather had bought from the member's only shopping club in town. Olivia reached for the bottle and shook two tablets into her hand. After she swallowed them down, she repeated the process with two more.

When she emptied the glass, she headed into the bathroom and relieved herself. She ran a brush through her hair, spent two minutes brushing her teeth, then entered the bedroom. Olivia had half a thought of putting last night's pajamas on, but she spotted a neatly folded pair of sweatpants on the dresser and slid those on. To her outfit, she added a T-shirt, and she returned to the door.

"Are you still there?" she asked.

"Yes," came the reply, muffled by the door.

Olivia unlocked the three locks, then opened the door a crack and looked outside.

"Are you alone?" Olivia asked.

"Yes," Torres said.

"Can you stand back against the wall?" Olivia asked.

Without answering, Torres took a step back until she felt the wall against her back. Olivia swung the door open a little wider, then stuck her head out. She looked both directions down the hallway, and seeing no one, stepped back into the apartment and opened the door wide.

"Come in, Detective," Olivia offered. "I'm sorry. What did you say your name is?"

"Torres. Gloria Torres."

Olivia didn't offer the detective a seat, instead she took her own spot on the stool at the kitchen island.

Olivia looked up and down at the woman. "You look familiar to me. Have we met?"

"Yes. At the police station a couple of weeks ago, when you had that incident at the grocery store."

Olivia thought for an extended minute, searching her memory. Slowly, the pieces fit together. "I thought that matter was closed. You said all the charges got dropped, and I was free to go."

"That matter is closed, Ms. Branch. I'm here about another matter."

"What?"

"What is your relationship with Virginia Parks?" Torres asked.

"Who?"

"Virginia Parks." Torres opened her phone, brought up a photo, and showed it to Olivia. Olivia took the phone, glanced at the picture, and handed it back.

"I've never seen her before."

"You sure?" Torres asked.

"Yes."

"Can you tell me where you were the last two days?"

"Right here. I'm here every day all day," Olivia said.

"Can anyone confirm that?"

"Yes. My friend Heather stays with me most nights. She comes after work and leaves in the morning."

"Is there anyone besides her?"

Olivia shook her head. "No."

"Don't you go out? A job?"

"I worked from home. I have… had… my own business. For a few months I've been on a medical leave dealing with some issues."

Torres nodded. "I know all about your issues, Olivia. I understand what you've been through."

A look of confusion passed over Olivia's face. "How?"

"When you went missing, I worked on your case. Your friend Heather was super persistent in finding you."

"Oh," Olivia said. She leaned over, grabbed the second stool, and slid it in front of Torres.

Torres took it as a sign and sat.

"Why didn't you find me?" Olivia asked.

"Can I shoot it straight with you?" Torres said.

Olivia nodded.

"Finding a missing person isn't at all like you see on the television shows. There's a lot of work involved. Generally, about eighty percent of missing adults get found within twenty-four hours, and ninety-five percent within a month, but in your case, there were extenuating circumstances that hindered the search."

"Like what?"

"They snatched you too cleanly and left no evidence behind. Once I found out where you were when you got abducted, I canvassed every business on the block around that restaurant, as well as around your car. I interviewed probably two-hundred people and looked at just as many hours of video footage from the area and came up with nothing. Since they didn't take your car, we couldn't trace that, and it held no helpful evidence when we examined it. The biggest obstacle was that they took you a hundred and fifty miles outside of the city. Had I known that I could have called in regional, state, and federal resources, but I didn't. Most abductions stay local. In your case, it would have been like trying to find a needle in an acre's worth of haystacks. Honestly, it keeps me up at night what you went through, and I'm sorry I couldn't help you more."

Olivia nodded. "I understand."

"Good. Olivia, please. What can you tell me about Virginia Parks?"

"Detective, I told you. I've never met a Virginia Parks."

"Okay. So how do you explain the text messages to her?"

Olivia looked Torres directly in the eyes. "What messages?"

Torres brought up another photo on her phone and passed it to Olivia. "All these messages. About meeting up at a bar not far from here. How did you meet her?"

Olivia got agitated, jumped from her stool, moved around the island, and poured another glass of water. "I'm telling you; I don't know her. How do you even know those messages are from me? I'm not the only Olivia in the world. And you can put anyone's name with any number."

"That's true. You got me there," Torres said. She held her hand out to take her phone back and discreetly pressed a couple of buttons before putting it back in her pocket.

Olivia lifted the glass to drink, then set it down when she overheard her phone ringing. Without excusing herself, she rushed to the bedroom to grab it. She picked it up, hit the green button, and put it to her ear. "Hello? Heather?"

"No, Olivia. It's me."

Olivia disconnected the call and threw the phone to the bed. When she turned around, she saw Detective Torres standing in the doorway.

Torres disconnected the call and placed her phone back in her pocket. "We're confident the messages came from you, because they came from the number I just called. The number you answered. It's your number, Olivia. Can I see your phone?"

Olivia shot forward and grabbed her phone from the bed and held it in both hands close to her chest.

"No. You can't. Don't you need a warrant or something?"

"Only if you're not going to cooperate. Are you going to cooperate with me, Olivia?"

Olivia stepped backward until she contacted the window. "No. Go away. Don't come back."

Detective Torres stood her ground.

"Go," Olivia repeated.

"I'll go. I'm going to get the warrant, and I'll be back."

Detective Torres turned to leave with Olivia right on her heels. Neither said another word. Once Torres was in the hall, the door slammed behind her, and she heard the locks getting engaged. She made her way down the hall and climbed down the stairs in no big hurry. When she got to her car, she looked up at Olivia's apartment. She saw the curtains move, so she assumed Olivia had eyes on her. Once in the car, she got out her phone and placed a call to the station.

"Hey, it's Torres. Did you get the information back on Olivia Branch that I want? Yeah, I'll hold." While she waited, Torres turned on the car and put on her seatbelt. "Yeah. I'm here. She has a prescription for what? Do you know if that's in the clonazepam family? Interesting. I'm headed back to the station now."

* * *

Olivia watched from behind the curtains as Detective Torres got into her car and kept her eyes on her the entire time she sat there. Only once Torres drove away did Olivia move away from the window.

She picked up a squeak and looked down. In his cage,

Nibbler was standing on his back legs with his little mouse arms reaching out to her. Olivia reached in, gently took hold of the mouse, and carried him to the couch.

"Why would she think I knew that Virginia, Nibbler? Did I? I'm here all the time. Where would I ever meet her?"

Nibbler squeaked, then gave Olivia a love nip on her finger. He jumped from her hand onto her leg, walked in a little circle, and laid down for a nap.

"What about the unaccounted times?" Daphne asked.

"What unaccounted times?" Olivia said, looking up. Daphne wasn't on the ground. Instead, today, she floated a foot above it.

"You're getting worse, Olivia. You really need to work the problem before this problem kills you."

"It's not even me. I'll bet it's Susie and Michael. They're setting me up. That's it."

"Or they might be sitting in prison right now," Daphne said.

"You think so?"

"Well, there's only one way to find out, isn't there?" After her last word, Daphne shimmered so brightly that Olivia had to shield her eyes with her arm. Then she disappeared.

Olivia rose and gently put Nibbler back in his cage. He lifted his head, recognized where he was, and put it down again to rejoin his mouse dream already in progress.

Olivia understood what she needed to do next. She just didn't want to do it. After thirty minutes of pacing around the apartment, Olivia raised enough courage to find the phone number of the sheriff's department. All she needed to do next was punch in ten numbers to make the call. The ten digits seemed easy enough, but when it came to pushing the green button to call the number, she couldn't do it. Time after time, she'd get close, but not close enough to actually make the call.

Olivia did a few more laps around the apartment.

"Have courage, Liv," she said. "Liquid courage!"

Olivia headed to the flower box and pulled the last fifth from the hiding place.

"My last one. Maybe I should save it."

She looked from the bottle to the phone. "I'll just have a little. Enough to get me through the call, and no more than that."

Olivia carried the bottle back to the kitchen and sat on her favorite stool. She put her phone on the island, opened the bottle, and drank a few gulps. Once she felt the warm liquid hit her stomach, she quickly put the numbers into the phone and hit the green button to connect the call.

It rang twice before someone picked up.

"Sheriff's Department. Please hold."

Before Olivia could say anything, she heard the dulcet tones of smooth jazz. She put the call on speaker mode, set it on the counter, and took a few more sips of vodka.

"Deputy Jameson. Thank you for holding. How can I help you?"

Olivia hesitated.

"Hello? Is anyone there?" the deputy asked.

Olivia took another drink to further steel her nerves.

"Can I speak to Deputy Becky?"

"This is. Deputy Becky Jameson. Who is this?"

"This is Olivia Branch calling. You probably don't—"

"Olivia! Of course I remember. You've been the talk of the county ever since Smitty picked you up. How have you been?"

A myriad of possible answers slipped through Olivia's mind, but the most convenient one was the lie she told herself. "I've been fine."

"That's good to hear. Why are you calling?"

"Could you tell me anything about the case? Like if you've caught Susie and Michael yet?"

Becky paused a good ten seconds before answering. "Hey, look, Olivia. I get off shift in a half an hour. Can I call you back? That way we can speak without me worrying about taking other calls and I can give you my undivided attention."

"I guess that sounds okay," Olivia said.

"If something happens, I'll send you a text to let you know I'll be late, but otherwise, I'll call you back in forty minutes. That will give me time to get home and take off my gun."

"Forty minutes. My number is —"

The deputy interrupted her and gave Olivia her own number. "We've got all the best equipment. I'll talk to you soon."

Deputy Becky killed the call without saying goodbye, and Olivia set the phone down on the counter and returned to her vodka bottle. She fully intended to nurse it since it was her last one, but even sips added up, and by the time the phone rang, it stood almost empty.

"Hello?" Olivia said.

"Hey, there. It's Becky. What do you want to know?"

"Can you give me an update on my case?" Olivia asked.

"I'm not supposed to, but because it's you, I will. Remember, though, the investigation is still ongoing, and some of this will probably go on for another year or more. What I can tell you is Susie and Michael have been on their murder spree for at least five years. So far, we've reunited the remains of fifty-nine missing women with their families. We've closed a lot of cold cases, thanks to you."

"There were that many women? Buried in the woods?" Olivia asked.

"In the woods, near the house, under the house, under the silo. And chances are there will be more. The forensic crews are all working overtime since we raided the farm, and even this many months later, we're still uncovering other remains."

Olivia shuddered. That could have happened to her. Just another missing person uncovered in the woods.

"The ID cards we found number in the hundreds, and we have a small team of people tracking those down. Fortunately for us, most of the women who owned them are still alive and were the victims of nothing more than light robberies or identity theft."

"That's good news, at least," Olivia said. "Do you have any information about Susie or Michael?"

"Not much. They disappeared like a fart in a hurricane. The only thing we're certain of is that the names they gave you aren't real. We've got agencies at every local, state, and federal level on the lookout for them. We've also alerted TSA, the border patrol, and the Canadian and Mexican governments to be on the lookout for them."

"Do you have pictures of them?"

"They both appear on the video we found of the cells, and I have to tell you, I regret even watching some of them. If you ask me, the best thing that could happen to them is to die in a hail of bullets, just like Bonnie and Clyde. Actually, they both deserve worse than that."

"Becky, do you think they'll come after me?" Olivia asked in a voice just above a whisper.

Becky hesitated a little too long, and Olivia heard an exhale over the line. "The best I can say is I hope not. If I were you, I'd get a gun and if you see either of them, shoot to kill. Are you sure you're okay?"

Olivia got her turn to hesitate. "I hope so."

"Call me if you need anything," Becky said. Again, without warning, she ended the call.

Olivia dropped the phone to the table. She swirled the liquid left in the bottle, then emptied it.

"Last one."

Olivia held the bottle in the air like it was a lost treasure, then let it slip from her grip. The plastic made a hollow thunk when it hit the island, and a second one when it landed on the floor. She crossed her arms on the island and put her head down. She felt like weeping, but a pounding on her door prevented her from doing so.

"Go away," she yelled. "There's no one home."

The rapping came again.

"Ugh," Olivia said as she got to her feet. She approached the door and looked through the peephole.

The hallway appeared empty, so Olivia undid all her locks and opened the door a crack. Again, she saw no one, but when she looked down, she spotted a brown paper bag in front of her door. She opened the door wide enough to drag the bag in, then closed and locked the door.

Olivia glanced into the bag and smiled. Within it sat six new bottles of vodka.

CHAPTER ELEVEN

Olivia glanced at her phone and the readout said it was eleven-fifteen. At first, she couldn't tell if it was night or morning, but a breeze came through the window, moved the curtains, and in doing so, let in enough of the pre-noon sunlight to let Olivia recognize she'd slept through most of the morning.

With some effort, she sat in bed. She sniffed and sensed something wasn't quite right. At first, Olivia thought it was her and tried to remember the last time she'd showered. Yesterday? The day before? She sniffed again. The scent that lingered in the air wasn't a body odor issue or someone who'd remained unwashed for several days. It was more reminiscent of a carton of spoiled milk left out in the scorching sun for too long.

Olivia felt overheated, and her pajama top stuck to her chest. When she attempted to pull it away from her skin, it stuck, and her fingers touched not the soft material of her pajamas, but a texture not unlike moist corn flakes that fell to a linoleum-covered table and dried there.

She rose and staggered into the bathroom and stared at her reflection in the mirror. At that point, she realized the problem.

During the night, or, more likely, during the morning after Heather left, Olivia had vomited. She had crusted vomit all over the front of her shirt, and dried remnants on her chin. She tried again to pull the garment from her torso, but it wouldn't budge. It remained stuck, as if Olivia had regurgitated an entire stomach's worth of the white paste she sampled when in kindergarten.

Olivia turned on the shower and dropped her pajama bottoms. While she waited for the water to warm, she brushed her teeth to get rid of the bile taste she had. When she noticed steam escaping from behind the curtain, she stepped in, letting the water cascade over her face and down her top. Once saturated, she peeled it from her flesh and dropped it outside the shower.

Thirty minutes later, Olivia returned to the bedroom and stepped into a set of fresh clothes. She moved to the window to collect a bottle from the flower box and the closer she got to the bed, the more prominent the smell of upchuck became. She discovered the source when she inspected the sheets. Not only had she made a mess on her shirt, she had dirtied the sheets and her pillowcase as well.

Olivia sighed as she stripped the sheets from the bed. She bundled them up and shoved them into the washing machine. Liv remembered her gross pajamas, added them to the machine, and started the washer.

She retrieved a bottle and wandered into the living room.

"Hey, you," she said to Nibbler, who was actually using his wheel for exercise rather than for a sleeping perch.

Nibbler stopped, exited the wheel, and did little mouse circles in his cage. He moved to his little food bowl and placed his front paws on the rim, as if to express displeasure that it was empty.

Olivia took the hint and extracted the dish.

"I'll be right back."

Olivia took the dish to the kitchen, rinsed it out, and opened the fridge. The container reserved for Nibbler's fresh fruits and vegetables had only dregs left in the bottom. She checked the refrigerator doors and found only a single carrot and a handful of strawberries. She piled those on the counter, and to it added a handful of trail mix from Heather's secret stash in the pantry.

"You do realize chocolate isn't good for mice," Daphne said.

Olivia looked up and spotted Daphne. "You've updated your look."

Daphne didn't shimmer, nor did she wear her favorite teacher outfit. Today she stood decked out in black from head to toe, dressed in a black suit, polished black leather shoes, a black shirt, and a long black tie. "It's a somber day. I've brought some people who want to talk to you."

"Can it wait? I need to feed Nibbler." Without waiting for a response, Olivia ate the chocolate candies from the trail mix, then dumped everything into Nibbler's bowl and carried it to his cage. "Your meal, my little furry friend," she said as she lowered the food. Nibbler squeaked with appreciation, then dug into the feast.

"Now, it's time," Daphne started.

Olivia wanted to give her a rude comment, but a buzzer from the washing machine interrupted her thought. Ignoring Daphne, she moved to the washer and found the out-of-balance light on. She opened the top, redistributed the sheets in the machine, and restarted the cycle. Olivia stayed a moment to ensure the machine wouldn't tilt again, then returned to the kitchen and her vodka bottle.

She broke the seal and took a swig. "Okay Daphne, why are you here looking all dour?"

"I brought someone to meet you."

As Olivia stared at Daphne, she began to shimmer. A slit appeared in the specter's midsection, and it widened and lengthened until it grew into a bright white door in the space where Daphne stood. Through the door stepped a young girl.

Olivia stepped back until she hit the stool, which tipped over and clattered on the floor. "Who are you?"

The girl took a second step. She wore dirty blue jeans and a pink blouse with the right sleeve torn off. One side of her long blond hair looked caked with mud. "You're Olivia?"

"Yes. Who are you?"

"Chloe."

"What happened to you?"

"You did."

"What? I don't understand. I don't know you."

"But I know you. I have heard everything about you. The one that got away. You didn't stop her, so she did this to me."

Chloe turned her head, and when she did, Olivia noticed the large hole in the side of Chloe's head, and what she'd taken for mud was actually blood.

Olivia put her hands to her mouth and turned her head away. "I didn't do that. I'm not responsible for you. Go away."

Olivia sensed a flash of light, and when she turned, Chloe had disappeared, and Daphne had returned.

"I didn't do that," Olivia said, pointing at the area Chloe had vacated.

Daphne didn't speak. Instead, she transformed once again into a door. As she watched, Olivia grabbed her bottle, took a long drink, and pulled it to her chest.

Another woman stepped through the door. This one had curly dark hair and deep brown, almost black eyes. Her Indian heritage was evident in her facial features. Like Chloe, she wore blue jeans but had no shirt. She seemed unaware of her nakedness and didn't try to hide her bosom. Olivia saw no flaws on any part of her exposed almond-tinted skin.

"I'm Anushka," she said as she stepped into the room. "I roomed with Chloe for a short time. A day or two. She was smart. She stayed silent. Me? I asked questions. When she told us about you, I asked questions. For details. It's my nature, and I paid for it."

Anushka turned around and exposed her bare back to Olivia. Olivia half-expected to see whip marks. What she saw was unspeakable.

"What happened to you?" Olivia asked.

Anushka turned back around. "They caught me on campus. I always studied late at the library. My father insisted that anything less than a perfect score was a failing score. Every night I closed the library, even though the route I took to my dorm was dark and deserted at that time. I don't know how long I was gone, but when I asked questions about you, it hastened my exit. They started with the whip, and when she grew bored with that, she switched to a hatchet. Now I don't know where I am, and my parents don't understand where I've gone."

"I'm sorry," Olivia said. The bottle fell from her hands. She picked it up and took a drink.

"You should be," Anushka said. "You didn't stop her. Olivia, you did this to me."

Tears fell from Olivia's eyes, and she rocked her head. "I didn't!" she screamed. "I couldn't have!"

Anushka shook her head as well, but she wore a look of disapproval rather than one of denial. After a moment, she faded away.

"Why are you doing this to me? I don't know these women," Olivia said.

"I'm not doing anything," Daphne said. "You are. Olivia, you have a problem. You need to work the problem."

Olivia drained the bottle. "I'll try to be clear. I don't have a problem!" She let out a primal scream, then threw her empty bottle at Daphne. It passed right through Daphne's incorporeal form and hit a clay pot holding Heather's favorite African Violet plant. Almost in slow motion, a pot shard dropped away, and the beautiful blooming plant followed to the floor, spraying dirt everywhere.

Daphne turned and glanced at the mess. "Heather is going to be so angry with you. You have another problem, Olivia. You're stacking them layer upon layer. Remember the steps from class? Identify the root cause of the problem, try a solution. If it doesn't work, try something else. Work the problem. Please, Olivia, for the sake of your soul."

Olivia closed her eyes. When she opened them a second later, Daphne had gone. Frustrated, Olivia went to her flower box and extracted another bottle, went back to her couch and drank half the bottle without pausing. She noticed a headache coming on, so she leaned her head back on the couch and closed her eyes.

When she opened her eyes, she saw Heather standing before her.

"What are you doing here?" Olivia asked.

"I thought I'd come by on my lunch hour and check on you. How are things going?"

"Good. I'm just doing some laundry."

Heather leaned over and pulled the half-empty bottle from Olivia's hand. "What's going on here?"

Olivia tried to snatch it back, but Heather was too fast for her. Since the bottle was already open, she took two steps back, inverted the bottle, and dumped the contents onto the bare floor.

"No!" Olivia screamed. She fell from the couch to the floor and pawed at the growing puddle.

"Olivia. Come on, get up," Heather said. She grabbed Olivia under the arms, helped her get to her feet, and placed her gently back on the couch.

Once Olivia got settled, Heather walked over to the remains of her plant. She moved the plant aside and brushed away a little dirt and picked up the bottle Olivia had used as a missile.

"Olivia. Where are you getting these from? Where are you hiding them?" Heather asked.

Olivia didn't answer, and instead looked at the floor.

"You need help, honey, please."

Olivia began to cry. "Daphne was right. You're mad at me."

A look of confusion passed over Heather's face. "Who is Daphne? Never mind. That doesn't matter. If I can get you in, can we go see Dr. Longstreet?"

"Today?" Olivia asked.

"I'd push for today. As soon as we can get in. Will you go?"

Olivia timidly nodded. "Are you mad at me?"

Heather sat on the couch and embraced her friend. "No, Olivia. I'm not. It may seem like I am, but I feel like I need to be firm with you to get you the help that you need. It comes from a place of love, though, not anger, okay?"

Olivia nodded again. "I'm sorry about your plant."

"Olivia. It's only a plant. We can get another. Okay. I'm going to go make a call. Do you think you can clean up a little?"

"Sure."

Heather pulled her phone from her pocket and left the room. While she was gone, Olivia retrieved the trash can from the kitchen and threw away her vodka bottles and used her hands to scoop up the dirt and tossed the broken pot and uprooted plant into the trash with her bottles. Next, she retrieved two kitchen towels and did her best to mop up the spilled vodka.

She was about to pull out the vacuum to take care of the rest of the dirt when Heather reentered the room.

"Forget about that. The doctor can see us as soon as we get there. Can you get dressed to go out?" Heather said.

Without answering, Olivia toddled down the hall and into her bedroom.

Heather felt relieved that Olivia hadn't noticed that she held one arm behind her, and when Olivia left the room, Heather stepped to the sink and drained the contents of the three vodka bottles into the sink. She added the empty bottles to the trash, closed and tied the bag shut, and placed it next to the door to take out when they left.

Thirty minutes later, Olivia, Dr. Longstreet, and Heather sat in a small circle in her office.

"…I don't know what she's talking about. I don't have a problem, and I'm in complete control of myself," Olivia said. She crossed her arms and leaned back in her chair, her body language more than expressing her defense.

"Can I show you something?" Heather asked.

"Sure," Dr. Longstreet said.

Heather leaned down and retrieved the laptop, propped against her chair leg. She opened it, clicked a few buttons and turned it around so Olivia and the doctor could see the screen. Heather pressed the play button and let the video roll.

Olivia appeared on the screen in the living room. She left the room and reappeared with a vodka bottle. As the video ran, the three watched as Olivia had an apparent argument with herself that ended in her throwing a bottle across the room and destroying a plant.

Heather paused the video, then called up another video. This one caught the image of Olivia sitting up in bed, vomiting on herself, then lying right back down and going to sleep. A third video showed Olivia retrieving bottles of vodka from her secret hiding place in the flower box.

After the third video played, Heather closed the laptop and set it down. She opened her mouth to say something, but the doctor held up a finger and stopped her.

"Olivia," Dr. Longstreet said, "Can you tell us about what you just saw on the video?"

"You spied on me?" she asked Heather.

"Olivia. All she did was follow my recommendations."

"She spied on me! In my own house!" Olivia sprung from her chair, causing Heather to recoil in hers. She took two steps toward Heather, then turned and headed for the door instead.

"Olivia," Dr. Longstreet said in a calm voice. "Please come back and join us."

Liv put her hand on the doorknob, and just as she did, the doctor stood.

"Olivia!" the doctor shouted.

Olivia froze, then looked back over her shoulder.

"Please, come back and join us."

Olivia dropped her hand to her side, then trudged back to her seat.

"All Heather did was do what I told her to do. We've suspected that you have a problem with alcohol, and these videos seem to confirm it. You're showing several symptoms of alcoholism, and it needs to be addressed."

"How? Do you want to have more sessions with me?" Olivia asked.

"At this point, what needs to happen is you need to get into a program to get you sober. Once you've taken care of that issue, then we can begin meeting again to work on your other issues."

"I'll go to other meetings?" Olivia asked.

"No," Dr. Longstreet said. "I'm recommending an inpatient facility for you. I took the liberty of calling a couple of places in town and found you a spot."

"What do you mean, a spot?"

"You'll stay there while you're getting sober," Dr. Longstreet said.

"Like overnight?"

"For as long as it takes for you to get sober."

Olivia shook her head. "No. I can't. Who would take care of Nibbler? He needs food and water."

"I'll take care of him," Heather said. "You know I will."

Olivia had no further questions, so Dr. Longstreet rose and got a piece of paper from her desk and handed it to Heather.

"Here's the address and the name of the person you should ask for when you get there."

Heather looked at the paper and put it in her pocket.

"Are you ready to get some help?" Heather asked.

"I suppose," Olivia said.

"Well, we'd better get a move on, then."

CHAPTER TWELVE

"Jimmy, we really need to stop meeting like this. That beautiful new bride of yours is going to become suspicious of us," Detective Torres said as she approached the doctor.

"Good morning, Gloria. Were your ears burning? We were talking about you last night. She said I should invite you over for dinner soon. This weekend or next, if you're free."

"Whose idea was that? Yours or hers?"

"Hers. She said since I talk about you all the time, you two should meet."

Gloria smiled. "Okay. I'll come to dinner, but it sounds like a trap to me, so I'm bringing my sidearm."

"It would genuinely surprise me if you didn't."

"Okay, so what do we have here?"

"Apparently, we got ourselves a dead body on the fifth green," the doctor said.

"Then why are we all here in the parking lot and not on the fifth green?" Torres asked.

"You will not believe this, but the groundskeeper doesn't want us to mess up the pristine fairways with our vehicles. From what I understood from Officer Press over there, the keeper was nice enough to give the responding officers a free golf cart to check it out, provided they stay on the marked path."

"You're shitting me," Torres said.

Dr. Seer shook his head.

"Press!" Torres yelled.

She waited while the officer jogged over to her.

"Yes, Detective?" the young recruit said. Torres could tell by the crispness of his uniform and the way he carried himself that he was fresh out of the academy and hadn't been with the department for more than a month.

"Why are we sitting here in the parking lot?"

"The groundskeeper won't let us through, Detective."

"Here's what's going to happen. I'm going with the doctor in his vehicle to the scene. Has the forensics unit been here yet?"

"No, Detective."

"When they arrive, you send them to the scene in their vehicle. Got it?"

"What about the groundskeeper?" Officer Press asked.

"Do you carry a pair of handcuffs on you?"

Press dropped his hand to his belt to feel for them.

"They're on the other side, Press. I can see them from here. If the groundskeeper gives you any further problems, you take those handcuffs from your belt and arrest him for obstruction. You can do that for me, can't you?"

"Yes, Detective," Press said.

"Good. Doctor, let's go."

The pair climbed into the doctor's wagon, and he threw it into gear and took off down the cart path.

"You were a little hard on the guy," Seer said.

"He'll thank me someday. He needs to learn how to take control of a scene and not let people walk all over him."

It didn't take long to get to the crime scene. Dr. Seer parked his wagon right behind the golf cart the officers used to arrive.

Torres jumped out of the wagon, and rather than ask her men for an update, she walked to the green. There, laying spreadeagled and face up, was a young woman who looked no more than twenty-three years of age. She was beautiful in a classical sense, with shoulder-length brown hair pinned back with one stray strand that covered her left eye. The emerald-green sleeveless dress she wore came respectfully to the knee, and she wore a string of pearls around her neck with a bracelet and earrings to match. Torres thought the woman reminded her of the stylish Audrey Hepburn. The two things that looked out of place were the woman wore no shoes to protect her pink-painted toes, and someone had positioned her, so her knees were on either side of the flagpole, as if it had sprung out of the ground beneath her. She also had a golf ball next to her left elbow.

"What do you think? Date gone wrong?" Dr. Seer asked.

"You already know what I think. Check her throat for me."

"I need to take the pictures first. Follow the protocol."

Torres waved at him impatiently. "I get it. Do what you need to do. If this is another serial, the pictures will be all we have. Forensics in all the other cases found literally nothing of value for the investigations. All of these cases seem like carefully planned and executed body dumps."

"But why?"

Torres shrugged. "I won't be able to tell you that until we catch the guy doing it."

While the doctor took his pictures, Torres meandered over to where the responding officers were taking statements from the early-morning duffers who had the unfortunate luck to get the first tee time of the day.

"I didn't mean to hit her," an elderly man in coral-checkered pants and a light blue polo shirt said. "I couldn't even see her over the ridge. All I could see was the top of the flag, so I aimed for that. I didn't kill her, did I?"

Torres noticed the doctor was ready to get to the important

part, so she left the men and rejoined her colleague.

She patted her pants pockets and realized she was missing something. "You got any spare gloves?"

Dr. Seer pointed his forceps at his backpack. "Front pocket. Help yourself."

Torres donned the gloves, then kneeled next to the victim. "Need any help on this one?"

"We'll see."

The doctor opened the mouth, and with little effort extracted the red balloon.

"I guess it's our guy," Torres said.

"You want to do the honors or should I?" the doctor asked as he dropped the balloon into a plastic bag.

"Go ahead. I can already guess most of it," Torres said.

Dr. Seer manipulated the balloon so he could read the writing. "I'm coming for you."

"What's the letter?" Torres asked.

"I."

"Do you hear that?" Torres said.

Seer tilted his head and listened for a moment. "Sounds like a vibration coming from her." The woman had no pockets, so he lifted the bottom of her dress.

"What are you doing?" Torres asked.

Rather than explain, Seer reached into the golf cup beneath the woman and extracted a cell phone.

"Magic trick," he said. He bagged the phone in plastic and handed it to Torres.

"Good trick," Torres said. She hit the side button, and the lock screen came up. "Bad news. This one has pattern security enabled and not a fingerprint one. I'll have to take it to the lab and see if they can crack it."

"She just got a call, right? Maybe you'll get lucky, and they'll call back. Then you can answer and find out who the phone belongs to."

"I'm impressed, doctor. You'd make a fine detective."

Seer shook his head. "Nope. Not me. I couldn't deal with the crazy hours."

Both people looked at the phone when it vibrated again. Without hesitation, Torres accepted the call and put it on speaker.

"Hello?" Torres said.

"Iva? Where are you?" the voice said.

"Who are you trying to reach?" Torres asked.

"Iva Parker. This is her number, and you're not Iva. Who is this?"

Without answering, Torres closed the call. "I for Iva."

"Iva's a unique name. She shouldn't be too hard to track down," Seer said.

"True, I think…" Torres looked glanced at the phone when it vibrated in her hand and connected the call. "Hello? Are you there? Hello?"

The call dropped, and Torres stared at Seer.

"Who was that?" Seer asked.

"My new best friend. Olivia Branch. Let's wrap this up. I have a warrant to serve."

* * *

Heather ran the vacuum cleaner over the spot for a second time where her African Violet had hit the floor, then bent over and ran her fingers over the rug. She felt a bit more grit, so she addressed the spot a third time. Finally satisfied, she expanded her range to cover the entire floor. Almost finished, she turned off the machine when she thought she heard a knock at the door.

"Who's there?"

Heather looked through the peephole and saw Detective Torres and two uniformed officers standing outside the door. She undid the locks and opened the door.

"Detective Torres. What brings you here?"

"I have a warrant to search the premises. Can you have Ms. Branch come out, please?"

"I could, but she's not here," Heather said.

"Where is she?"

"We checked her in to an addiction facility."

Torres nodded. "We'll talk about that later. We still need to search the apartment."

"I assume you'll let me see the warrant?" Heather said.

Torres nodded, then extracted it from her jacket pocket and handed it over. Heather took the paper, opened it, and read through the document without leaving the doorway. When she finished, she stepped inside and allowed the three officers to enter.

"Can you stay out here?" Torres asked.

"Sure," Heather said as she took a seat on the stool. "Would you mind not messing the place up too much?"

"You heard her. Go gentle. I'll start out here. You guys take the other rooms," Torres said.

Torres slipped on a pair of gloves and started in the kitchen.

"Can you tell me what you're looking for?" Heather asked. "I might be able to make things easier for you."

"No. You sit there and let us all do our jobs and we'll be out of your hair in no time," Torres said as she started working her way through the upper cabinets.

"Does this have something to do with the incident at the grocery store?" Heather asked.

Torres scoffed. "We closed that case, and even if we hadn't, it's small potatoes in comparison."

She stayed silent as she rummaged through the cabinets in the kitchen, then moved on to under the sink, and all the appliances, going as far as making sure every can and boxed item in the small pantry was authentic, and each item in the refrigerator was actually what it was supposed to be.

"Detective?" one officer called from the back room.

"Wait here, please," Torres said to Heather.

Heather sighed and drummed her fingertips on the countertop. She got up, retrieved a bottle of water, and returned to her seat. She nursed the water, cleaned out the email on her phone, answered a text, and waited for an eternity. Heather was busy reading about an art exhibition coming to town when Torres returned to the room.

On the island, Torres dropped two plastic evidence bags.

"What do you have there?" Heather asked, setting down her phone.

"This," Torres said, picking up one of the evidence bags, "is a ten-pack of red balloons, and this is a prescription bottle."

Heather shook her head. "I don't see what the big deal is. Party balloons and medicine?"

Torres pulled out the other stool and sat next to Heather. A moment later, the two officers entered the room and worked their way through the living room.

"We've got a wet stain over here, Detective," an officer reported.

Heather turned around and looked at where he stood. "That's vodka. I caught Olivia with a bottle and dumped it out right there in front of her."

"Get a sample for analysis," Torres said.

The officer used a swab to gather a sample and put the swab into a small tube. He put the tube in an evidence bag, sealed and tagged it, and added it to the small pile on the island. When they pulled the couch away from the wall, they discovered four empty vodka bottles. All got bagged, tagged, and added to the growing haul.

The officers found nothing else, so Detective Torres dismissed them. When the door shut, Torres turned to Heather.

"Your friend is in some serious trouble."

"What kind of trouble? Was there something else she did in a drunken state she wasn't aware of? Is she having fights with non-existent people I don't know about? Throwing things at people? What?"

"What do you mean by the fights?"

Heather retrieved her laptop and booted it up. "I assumed Olivia had a problem with alcohol, but I didn't understand how large a problem it was. Since she rarely leaves this apartment, her therapist suggested I set up cameras to keep an eye on her. Here's some footage from yesterday."

Heather played the clips for the detective, who watched with interest.

"Do you have any other video of her?" Torres asked.

"No. Yesterday was the first time I had the cameras up and running. My biggest mystery is figuring out how she is getting the vodka. Like I said, she rarely goes out. It's all I can do to convince her to take the trash to the chute or walk down the stairs to get the mail."

"Did you find your answer?"

"No. I discovered her hiding place, though. She stashed it in the flower box outside the bedroom window. I wouldn't have thought to even look there had I not seen it on the feed."

"How long has she been drinking?" Detective Torres asked.

"Honestly, I don't know, but I think it started almost immediately after we got her back."

"Do you know if she's drinking to the point of blacking out or going into fugue states?"

Heather uncapped her water and took a drink. "Again, I'm not sure. I've been staying over every night since she got back. Olivia has trouble sleeping, and often had night terrors. She even sleeps with the lights on, which is totally annoying for me. I think she waits until I leave in the morning and drinks all day, every day."

"Where do you go?" Torres asked.

"To run my normal life. I have a job I need to do, and my own apartment I need to upkeep. I also do most of the outside chores that need to be done. Grocery shopping, trips to the post office, or whatever. It's almost like I'm running two households."

"Why don't you take her out with you?" Torres asked.

"I tried. Olivia has way too much anxiety. Everywhere we go, she's convinced that someone is following her."

"Who?"

"Susie and Michael, of course."

"Have you ever seen them?" Torres asked.

"Nope. When she points them out, by the time I've turned around, they've mysteriously disappeared. One time I looked, and Michael turned out to be a bush."

"You said something about a therapist? Is she seeing one?"

"She is. The doctor is supposed to be helping Olivia through her emotional trauma, but the alcohol problem has sidelined that therapy. After today's session, the doctor recommended we put Olivia into a treatment center, so we did."

"Which one?"

"The Jordan Center. Down on Fifth Avenue."

Torres nodded. "That's a good one. She'll get the help she needs there."

"Okay. I've been more than helpful. You want to tell me what's going on?" Heather said.

Torres signed. "Understand that this is an ongoing investigation, and nothing I'm about to say is out in the public. I'm going to trust you that it's going to stay under wraps."

"Of course," Heather agreed.

"Over the last ten days, I've investigated the deaths of four different young women. The cause of death for each one was asphyxiation. A balloon shoved down their throats to be specific. They choked to death. Every balloon has a message written on it, along with the first initial of the woman's name."

Torres leaned over and grabbed the package of balloons. "Each of the balloons looked just like these."

"Those are pretty common. Those were probably leftover

from a birthday party we had."

"Maybe. My forensics team will tell me if it's a match. A little more incriminating is this." Torres picked up the bag containing the medicine bottle. "Each of the women got drugged with what is essentially a date-rape drug that makes them sleepy and prone to suggestion."

"Come on, Detective. Are you telling me that sweet little Olivia is going around drugging and killing women? Why? What's the motive?"

"In her case, there might not be one. I've seen it before. Someone who suffers a lot of psychological trauma disassociates with their natural self and does heinous things. Add to that enough vodka to fill a bathtub, and she may not even know she's doing it."

Torres picked up the bottle and looked at the information. "The prescribing doctor isn't on here. Do you know who it might be?"

"I would imagine it's Dr. Trish Longstreet. She's the therapist Olivia is seeing. Although…"

"What?" Torres said when Heather trailed off.

"Although I don't know how she could have filled the prescription. I didn't pick it up for her, and I'm fairly confident she wouldn't have gone out and gotten it herself. What pharmacy is that from?"

Torres read the information off the label.

"Yeah, no way. She would need to go right past five other pharmacies to get to that one. There's no way she would have done that," Heather said.

"She could have had it delivered," Torres said.

Heather nodded. "That's possible."

"I'll track down that lead, of course. The pharmacy will have records and may have her on video picking it up. Likewise, I plan on following up with the therapist."

"You can follow up all the leads you like," Heather said.

"But as far as Olivia is concerned, they will all come to a dead end. It's just not in her personality to do the things you're accusing her of."

"Why not?" Torres asked.

"She's just not the type. I can't imagine her doing such a thing."

"Well, could you ever imagine Olivia living in a silo in complete darkness for weeks? Living with little food and water? Then digging her way out by hand before getting in a brawl, resulting in her breaking her ribs and then walking almost a mile before finding help?"

Heather thought it over before answering. "Before it all happened, had we been drinking tea and coming up with wild scenarios to escape from, I would have said no. There's no way I would have guessed she would survive all that. But, now that she has, I admit she impressed me with how much grit and desire to survive she had. Right down to saving that little mouse."

"What you're telling me is, you're not really sure of what your friend is really capable of."

CHAPTER THIRTEEN

Olivia sat on the edge of her bed, fully dressed, her pillow clutched to her chest. There were three other beds in the room, two sets of bunk beds. Each bunk had a person assigned to it, and deep in the night, only Olivia remained awake. She requested they leave the lights on, and her roommates quickly scoffed at the suggestion. Next, she requested a night light, and that only prompted teasing from the three other women as well. When lights out came, Olivia tried to adapt by ducking under her covers and turning on the flashlight function of her phone. All that did was to drain the battery and leave her once again in the dark. She threw the covers off, sat up, and spotted the hallway light beaming in under the closed bedroom door.

When she'd had enough of staring at the slim sliver of light, she crept to the door and opened it. Although Olivia wanted it to open as silent as a whisper, the door emitted a loud creak the entire way. Olivia stopped and looked behind her, waiting for her roommates to rouse, but none did.

Olivia stepped into the hallway, then descended a flight of stairs. She spotted the front door, took a step toward it, then stopped when she overheard the television at the admission desk change channels. From the desk to the front door was only about eight feet, but she didn't know if they would catch her before she got there, or if they would even care.

"Where are you going?"

Olivia spun around, expecting someone on the staff, but instead she spotted Daphne, who was back to wearing her favorite teacher outfit.

"Shh, they'll hear you," Olivia said.

"How in the world could they? I'm only in your head. Here, watch."

Daphne took a deep breath, then screamed. To Olivia, it was so intense she bent over and pressed her hands to her ears. Daphne's yell was so blistering, Olivia could see the sound waves that came from Daphne's mouth.

Daphne stopped, then waited a moment. "See. No one heard me. Why? Because I'm only a part of your imagination."

"Well, be quiet anyway. You're freaking me out," Olivia whispered.

"Sure. Fine. But back to my original question. Where are you going?"

"Where does it look like? I'm leaving."

"Then why don't you simply walk past the front door? This is a voluntary facility. You can leave at any time," Daphne said.

"Yeah, well, maybe. I still don't want to be questioned about it."

Olivia turned around and started to explore the first floor. They'd given her a tour when she first arrived at the building, which had once been a three-story house, but she had paid little attention to it. All she remembered was where the kitchen was and that if food in the fridge had someone's name written on a label, you weren't supposed to touch it.

The first door she came to had a lock and deadbolt, and since it had a hand-printed sign on it that said 'office', it didn't surprise her. The next door was a bathroom. Since it stood wide open, Olivia stepped inside. The space was on the smaller side and contained only a toilet and a sink. The showers were on the second and third floors, where all the residents had rooms, women on the second floor, men on the third. Above the sink was an unbreakable mirror. She gave half a thought to wiggling out the bathroom window, but when she went to open it, she discovered it wouldn't budge, regardless of how hard she pushed.

Leaving the bathroom, she turned right and entered the kitchen. It was as she remembered, except there were two refrigerators instead of one. Two microwaves were present as well, one installed above the stove and one on a cart. The only window in the room was directly over the sink, and Olivia had no desire to crawl over the drying dishes to check its status.

She opened a fridge and found a small container of chocolate milk inside. Although the note on it said it belonged to Lana, Olivia took it out, opened it up, drank half right from the carton. When she finished, she wiped her mouth with her sleeve and returned the milk to where she found it. Satiated, she plodded across the hall into the dining room. A large wood table for eight sat in the center, and the room sides had tables pushed against the wall. On one was a small desk lamp. It was on, and the dim bulb illuminated a jigsaw puzzle in progress.

On the far wall was a row of six windows. She selected one at random, unlocked the sash, and rotated the crank near the sill. The window opened freely and without sound. Olivia leaned out and looked down. In the moonlight, she spotted a row of rose bushes beneath her.

"If you're looking to go, I'd use this one," a voice said. "And use the window. Don't even bother with the back door."

Olivia looked to her right and at the window farthest from her. At first, she noticed nothing, then spotted the glow of a cigarette brighten, then dim.

"Why?" Olivia asked.

"If you go out back, the only way out is to climb the far fence. That neighbor owns the meanest dogs ever born. If you jump from there, you'll land in those thorns. You leave from here, there's nothing but soft dirt below you."

"What makes you think I want to leave?" Olivia asked.

The woman took another drag on her cigarette and blew the smoke out the open window. "I've been here three months. It's not unusual for newbies to decide they don't want to be here. Most use the front door, though. Why don't you use the front door?"

"Why do you care?" Olivia asked.

The woman shrugged in the shadows. "I don't. Just curious."

"Because they'll ask questions, and I'm tired of being questioned."

"Well, then, here's your opportunity. Jump out the window and be free, little bird."

Olivia moved to the window and looked out. Like the woman had said, there was nothing below it to hinder her escape. Olivia pulled a chair from the dining table and put it beside the window. She stepped on the chair, using its back for balance, and stepped onto the sill.

"You just going to take the metaphorical leap?" the woman asked. "That's like a six-foot drop. I hope your knees are in good shape."

Olivia looked out the window again. As a kid, she would have jumped without question, but being older, she had her doubts that her body would react the same way. Her hand went to her side, and she considered how the impact would affect her ribs. Her surgeon had warned her against doing anything too strenuous, and she doubted jumping from buildings would have been on his list of approved activities.

"Do you have another suggestion?" Olivia asked.

"Go out legs first. I'll hold your arms and lower you down as far as I can. At most, the fall will be only a foot or so."

"You'll help me?"

The woman shrugged again. "Why not? I've got nothing better to do than a jigsaw puzzle that's missing twelve pieces."

"How do you know that?" Olivia asked.

"Because I do the same one every night. Last week I was missing only eleven pieces, and the week before ten, so I think someone is playing a little joke on me. I'll find out who it is, eventually. Then I'll get my revenge."

Olivia turned around in the chair and lowered her legs over the side. She moved out the window an inch at a time, holding onto the chair and then the windowsill. When she thought she might run out of things to hold on to, the woman grabbed Olivia's wrists and lowered her.

"You ready?" the woman asked.

"Let me go," Olivia said.

She dropped and landed immediately. The drop was no worse than going down a step.

"Are you okay?" the woman asked.

"Perfect. Thanks. Oh, hey, what's your name?"

"Lana."

"Thanks again, Lana. Oh, and sorry for drinking your milk."

Olivia moved to the corner of the house, saw the street seemed deserted, picked a direction, and started walking. When she arrived at the first street corner, she took a moment to get her bearings, complicated by not knowing where she wanted to go. Finally, she decided on home, turned left, and headed up the street.

She walked for an hour before she saw the parking lot lights of the grocery store that she got banned from. The perimeter of the lot had a knee-high brick wall around it, and when she reached it, Olivia sat on the wall to rest. She looked behind her nervously, expecting a full contingent of store security mixed with local S.W.A.T. to arrest her the second she touched store property, but instead all she noticed was a young man rounding up carts while talking on the phone.

Olivia put her hand on the wall and leaned over to stretch out her aching back. She discovered an untied shoe and took care of that chore. Behind her, she heard a crash of metal on metal, jumped up and looked in that direction. At first, she was relieved to see that the sound had come from the man pushing a long line of carts into a cart corral, but then she looked beyond him and caught the glance of a figure standing off to the side of the front door. She knew who it was immediately.

Olivia watched the figure as she started speed walking up the sidewalk toward her apartment building. She kept an eye on him. Based on the way he rotated as she made her way along, he was keeping an eye on her, too. She only had a few blocks to go, so Olivia took off in a slow jog. Since the streets were empty, she didn't need to worry about running into pedestrians, but in this situation, she'd almost welcome a crowd.

Olivia looked behind her. The man was jogging behind her, and although she'd had a head start, she only had a fifty-foot lead on him. She approached an intersection and ran across the street without bothering to check any direction for traffic. Behind her, she heard footfalls on the pavement, so she picked up her pace, even though her ribs ached, and she was gasping for breath. She smiled when she spotted her building and was about to run across the street when she saw the police car parked in front. Not wanting to attract attention, she slowed to a walk and kept going. Olivia no longer perceived the footsteps behind her, so she spun around and discovered whoever was following her had disappeared. Knowing she couldn't go home, Olivia turned left at the next corner and headed for the all-night laundromat two blocks away.

* * *

Detective Torres arrived at the Jordan Center ready to serve her warrant on Olivia to confiscate her phone. She got out of her car and was about to walk up the front steps when another car honked at her. Torres turned and watched as Dr. Seer double-parked his wagon right next to her cruiser.

"Were you in the area? It seems I always beat you to the scene," Dr. Seer said as he joined her on the stairs.

"I didn't get a call. I'm here to serve papers."

"Oh, that's right. The call came up as a probable accident. Not quite your department."

The detective rang the bell, and the door opened a moment later.

On the other side was a six-foot skinny bald man with a bushy mustache. He wore jeans an inch too short, and a black cardigan sweater a size too large. "I'm Davis Clark, the manager of this facility. You are?"

"Dr. James Seer. I'm with the medical examiner's office."

"Detective Gloria Torres."

"Lana is this way," Davis said. He turned around and waved for them to follow. He led them through the ground floor and into the dining room. "She's over there," he said, pointing at the far window.

Seer and Torres walked to the window. Seer looked over the edge of the window. Below him was the crumpled body of a woman. At first glance, she looked like she was in mid-somersault. Her head and back were on the ground, her legs leaned against the house.

"I'm headed outside," Dr. Seer said, then excused himself from the room.

"You're not going with him?" Davis asked.

"I'm actually here on another matter," Torres said.

"Really? What's that?"

"I need to see Olivia Branch."

Davis let out a long sigh. "I should have known. You can't see her. She's not here."

"What do you mean?"

"She ran away from the facility last night."

"You're kidding. When?"

"I'd have to check the footage for sure, but some time after the nightly bed check."

"Detective?"

Torres moved over to the window and glanced out. "Yes, doctor?"

Seer stood, stepped back, and ran his shirtsleeve over his forehead. "I think you should come out and join me. And you'll need to call in your forensics team."

Torres was by the doctor's side in a minute.

"Look there," he said, pointing. Torres followed his finger. Beneath the woman's shoulder was a heel print facing the house. "There are a couple of other prints around the body. I assume you need to preserve those tracks?"

"Not with the body on top of them. Did you get all the pictures you need?"

"As much as I could without moving her."

"Do you think we could move her together?" Torres asked.

Seer stepped to the side of the body and analyzed the situation. "I can't imagine she weighs more than one-twenty. If we got on either side of her and lifted straight up, I think we could pull her out without messing with the scene. Either way, I think it's worth a try."

Torres nodded, then took a position beside the body, careful not to step on any prints or obvious evidence. "How are we going to do this?"

"Based on her position, I think we should lift her by the belt, hope she doesn't slide out of her pants, and bring her straight forward. Hold on, I'll lay down a sheet."

From his pile of equipment, Seer donned a pair of gloves,

then unfolded a white sheet and laid it flat on the grass. He walked back to his position and told hold of the body.

"Ready?"

Torres grabbed the victim by her belt. "Let's do it. Go."

Together they lifted the woman, walked her slowly forward, and positioned her so she lay face up on the sheet.

"Was this an accident?" Torres asked. "Any signs of foul play?"

Dr. Seer gave the body a once-over. "I won't know for sure until I do a full autopsy. I can tell you she has a significant crack on the back of her head."

Dr. Seer gently touched her skull. "Yeah, she feels like a broken egg back here."

Torres walked back and examined the wall. "There's a lot of blood here. It certainly looks like she smashed her head on the concrete. Perhaps she was leaning out the window and she fell out?"

She turned her attention from the wall to the ground. She spotted something and squatted. "There's a cigarette here. She could have been taking a smoke break and fell."

"Excuse me, Detective, could you come and look at something with me?" Davis said from the window above.

"Sure. I'll be right in," Torres said. She inspected the field for other bits of evidence, but other than the bloodstain, the cigarette, and the footprints, she spotted nothing of use.

"Jimmy, I need to go talk to the guy. I'll be right back."

Seer waved, not taking his eyes off the body.

Torres made her way around the house, and when she entered, she found Davis in the office. When she knocked on the door, he stood and welcomed her in.

"Please, have a seat in my chair there," he said.

Torres sat, and Davis leaned on a file cabinet. "I have some video footage I'd like you to see." He leaned over and punched a button on his computer. The screen came to life, and Torres recognized the dining room.

"When is this from?" Torres asked.

"Last night. Watch."

A second later, Lana entered the room. She wandered over to the side table, turned on the light, and opened the puzzle box. David fast-forwarded the footage, and at double-speed, Lana worked on the puzzle in record time. He returned to normal speed when Lana stepped to the window, opened it, and lit a cigarette. A minute later, Olivia entered the room, and Torres watched her from the time she entered the room, until the time Lana lowered her out the window.

"Thanks. This was helpful," Torres said and moved to get up.

"Wait. There's more."

Torres returned to the screen and watched Lana stand up, then thirty seconds later, she leaned out the window again to toss the cigarette. In a second, she got yanked out of the room.

"Do you have audio on this?" Torres asked.

"No. Just video."

"I'll need a copy of this," Torres said.

"It's on the cloud. I'll make a copy of the file and send it to you."

Torres stood and rejoined the doctor. "We need to get the forensics team out here. This wasn't an accident. I think it's a homicide."

Dr. Seer looked up and frowned. "I know."

From the ground, he picked up an evidence bag and held it out. "It was in her mouth, but the head injury was most likely the cause of death. It's the same message as the others. I'm coming for you."

"And the letter?"

"L. For Lana," Seer said.

"Jimmy, we need to find Olivia Branch."

CHAPTER FOURTEEN

"Hey, wake up,"

Olivia felt a nudge on her shoulder and came awake with a start. She didn't mean to fall asleep, but eventually did. There was one other patron using the laundromat during the night, and Olivia talked to her for a while before the woman mentioned something about stepping out for a moment. The woman started the dryer before she walked away, and the tumbling rhythm combined with her exhaustion put Olivia right to sleep.

"You're not supposed to sleep here," the man said.

Olivia looked up and discovered a young Hispanic man next to her. Since he was leaning on a broom, Olivia assumed he was the custodian.

"I just fell asleep for a minute. It's been a long night," Olivia said.

"You homeless? You're not supposed to be here. I'm surprised the night manager didn't kick you out."

"No. I'm not homeless." Olivia spotted the woman's empty white plastic laundry basket on a table near the dryers. "See, my stuff is in that dryer right there. Like I said, I only closed my eyes for a moment."

To prove her point, Olivia opened the dryer and placed an armful of clothes on the table. There was a mishmash of items there. Socks, T-shirts, shorts, underwear, all in one load. When she used a coin operated laundry, she often combined loads herself to save money on the dryer. Olivia made a show of folding shirts and matching socks. The custodian watched her for a while and returned to sweeping the floor and emptying the lint traps and trash cans.

Once he left her view, Olivia returned to where she'd fallen asleep in the chair. She'd found a phone charger in the lost and found and used it to juice up her cell. She checked the battery life, discovered it at a hundred percent, and tucked the phone and the charger into her jeans pocket.

Olivia returned to the laundry pile, rummaged through it and picked out a clean T-shirt and a dark blue sweatshirt. She entered the single-stall bathroom, stripped out of the sweat-stained shirt she wore, rinsed herself in the sink, and put on the clean shirt. It was a size too large, and it ended at mid-thigh. Olivia tucked the excess into her pants, decided it looked too puffy, and extracted a couple of inches. It still looked silly, so she put on the sweatshirt and left the bathroom, tossing her old shirt into the trash as she passed it.

From the laundromat, she walked toward her apartment. The patrol was gone from right in front of her building, but a replacement was now parked directly across the street. She put the hood up, shoved her hands in her pockets, and walked by, hoping not to draw attention to herself.

As she passed, she glanced inside the police car. An officer sat in the driver's seat, working on a cup of coffee and occasionally glancing at her building. Once she cleared the car, she picked up her pace.

Olivia turned right at the next street and passed a line of row houses before she turned left and crossed the avenue. There, she found a bus stop, and she stepped inside the small shelter and sat on the metal bench.

She pulled her phone from her pocket, checked the time, and exhaled when she saw it was before seven in the morning. Olivia's phone case contained four slots to hold cards. The first three contained a credit card, a debit card, her driver's license, and her library card. The fourth was where she stashed her cash. Usually, she kept two twenties folded neatly in there, but when she extracted the money, she found only a single bill. She stared at it, hoping Lincoln's face would magically transform into Franklin's, but it didn't.

"You're not going to get far on five dollars," Daphne said.

"There's a bank a couple of blocks over. I can take some cash out of the ATM," Olivia said.

"Then what? Are you going to live on the mean streets like a fugitive?"

"No. The police will stop looking for me, eventually. Afterward, I can go back to my life."

"Why do you think they're here in the first place?"

"Probably because I left that facility last night."

"That makes no sense," Daphne said as she floated through the heavy Plexiglas wall and into the shelter. "It's a voluntary facility. They didn't commit you there. You could have left anytime you wanted to."

"Well, then it has to do with the grocery store thing," Olivia said.

She looked down at the five in her hand and stood. "Let's go, Daphne."

"Where to?"

"Get some cash and some breakfast."

Olivia stopped at the bank and withdrew a hundred dollars from the cash machine. From the bank, it was a six-block hike to the nearest donut shop. She selected a jelly-filled and ordered a large bourbon pecan roasted coffee to wash it down. Olivia took the donut and the coffee to a table and started eating the pastry as slow as possible and nursing the cup to make it last. Once she finished, she noticed the staff eyeing her impatiently until she stepped to the counter and ordered a regular black coffee with cream and Splenda and a glazed old-fashioned donut.

She returned to the table and again wasted as much time as she could with the meal. Olivia checked the hour on her phone, determined she'd milked as much time away as she could. She left the donut shop and wandered to the park across the street. There, she found a bench and made herself comfortable.

Olivia had a good view of the park from her bench. Since it was a school day, the playground was empty, but the squirrels running from tree to tree and chasing down nuts provided more than ample entertainment for her. She dozed, and when she woke Olivia discovered more action in the park. A group of people, numbering around thirteen, had assembled in the grass and were currently working through yoga poses in unison.

Olivia checked her phone and saw the time was a quarter past noon. She was about to shove her phone back in her pocket when she noticed the group chat was active.

Olivia opened the app and read back through the long string of messages.

Heather started the conversation, giving the group an update on Olivia's condition and asking the group if anyone had seen her. All her friends checked in at some point. Gabby only a few seconds after Heather's initial post. Tina and Michelle each chimed in a couple minutes later, and Sarah didn't respond for a good fifteen minutes with only a two-word response.

"What's going on?" Daphne said.

"They're talking about me. Wondering where I've gotten off to. Has anyone seen me, blah, blah."

"They're concerned about you."

"Blah. It's all gossip is what they're doing."

"Why don't you jump in on the chat? At least tell everyone

you're okay, even if you don't want them to know where you are?" Daphne said.

"Why? They don't really care about me. Let's go find something to drink."

Without waiting for Daphne to respond, Olivia left her bench and walked the four blocks to the supermarket. Before she got to the store, she put up the hood on the sweatshirt with a plan of sneaking in, grabbing the goods, and leaving with no problems.

When she reached the walled perimeter, she paused, took a deep breath, and went for it. Olivia walked through the parking lot like she belonged there, and the closer she got to the front door, the more confident she became.

The automatic door slid open when she approached. She stepped aside to let an elderly woman pass with a cart full of bags, then stepped into the store. Acting casually, Olivia grabbed a cart and wheeled it forward. She'd made it almost to the first display of red apples in the produce section of the store when a large man stepped in front of her cart and put his hand out to stop her. The man looked like a bear in a blue sweater vest, complete with a shaggy, long brown beard.

"You're not allowed in here. You're banned," he growled.

"I only need a couple of things. Please let me pass," Olivia said.

He didn't let go of the cart, and instead pushed it back into her. "You've got two choices. Leave of your own accord, or I'll have the police come and get you."

Without argument, Olivia let go of the cart and put her hands up in surrender. She took two steps backward, then pivoted and left the store in a rush.

"That didn't work like I hoped it would," Olivia said as she removed the hood from her head.

"Now what?" Daphne asked.

"Plan B, of course."

Olivia walked down the street and came to her neighborhood bodega. She headed right for the counter upon arrival. Plan B worked out well, for in a couple of minutes, Olivia traded two twenties for two bottles of vodka and a bag of pretzel rods. Out of habit, she began walking toward her apartment, then changed her mind and returned to the park.

When she arrived back at her bench, she noticed the yoga people had gone. In their place were two people in their mid-forties. They had laid out a blanket and were busy setting up a picnic from the fanciest picnic basket Olivia had ever seen. From it, the blond-haired woman extracted two glasses, plates, and silverware, while the blond-haired man struggled to open a bottle of wine. Olivia watched as the woman produced food items and distributed them on plates. Once the man poured the wine, they started to eat. Olivia couldn't hear the conversation, but occasionally, one or the other would erupt with laughter.

"What's going on?" Daphne asked.

Olivia removed a bottle of vodka from her paper sack, cracked the seal, and had a long drink. "Picnic. I didn't even know people still had picnics."

"He's quite smitten with her," Daphne said. "He's almost neglected his food completely and is hanging on every word she's saying."

Olivia took a drink of vodka at the same moment the woman took a drink of wine.

"Look, I think he's making a move," Olivia said. She watched as the man put down his plate. He leaned toward the woman and gently pushed the hair back from her eyes and moved in for a kiss. Rather than a primal, forceful kiss, it appeared more intimate than passionate.

"Aw, how sweet," Daphne said.

"Sure. If you think romance is sweet," Olivia said. She grew bored watching the couple, then fished her phone out of her pocket. She had another drink of vodka while she brought up the messaging app to scan for any updates.

"Hey, look at this. They all plan on getting together at that bar up the road from my place. What's the name of that dive? Frederick's? Finnigan's? Fernando's? It doesn't matter. Oh, the irony of them meeting at a bar to talk about what a lush I've become."

"I'm sure that's not the case," Daphne said. "Your friends are worried about you. You should call them now and tell them where you are and that you're okay."

"Actually, I've got a better idea. I'm going to sit here all afternoon, drinking my medicine and eating these pretzels, and when the time comes, I'll make a personal appearance, and we'll see how happy they really are to see me."

Olivia carried out her plan and, over the course of the day, she worked through a bottle and a half of the vodka and ate the entire bag of pretzels. Every hour she needed to use the restroom, so she left her bench and cut across the grass to use the park's facilities. Each subsequent time she did, she found the walk harder to do.

At six, she started her eight-block walk to the bar, and by six-thirty, she pulled open the door and lurched through. She stopped just inside the bar and saw her friends at a table not far away.

As Olivia got closer, Gabby said something, and the other women laughed.

"I see you're all having a good time," Olivia said.

"Olivia!" Heather screeched. "Where have you been?"

"Away," Olivia said. "So, what's so funny? Are you all talking about me? About how I've lost my marbles and spun out of control?"

"Of course not," Gabby said. "We're all worried about you."

"Really," Olivia said. She moved around the table to where there was an open seat. It was a high-top table, and Olivia struggled to climb the seat, but Michelle grabbed Olivia by the arm and helped her shimmy into the chair.

"Really," Gabby said.

"Is that why you've all been beating down my door trying to see me?" Olivia said. "You don't really care. And I'm positive that even Heather has gotten sick of me, and that's why she sent me off to that place."

"Olivia, that's not true. We decided together it was good for you to go there. Don't you remember? You and me and Dr. Longstreet?"

"You are all trying to put me away. I know it," Olivia argued.

"Here," Sarah pushed her glass of water in front of Olivia. "Drink this. You'll feel better."

"No," Olivia said.

Sarah leaned over and put her hand on Olivia's shoulder. Olivia flinched and slapped Sarah's hand away.

"Ow," Sarah said.

"Don't touch me," Olivia hissed.

"What's your deal, Liv?" Tina asked. "Are you drunk?"

"Maybe. But even if I wasn't, I don't want her to touch me." Olivia pointed directly at Sarah's chest. Her bloodshot eyes narrowed, and her brow furrowed as she stared at her ex-friend.

"What did I do?" Sarah asked.

"You really don't want to know," Olivia said.

"I do. You're clearly upset with me. Tell me why." Sarah leaned closer to Olivia so that Olivia's outstretched finger touched Sarah in the middle of her breastbone.

"You can't even imagine why," Olivia growled.

Sarah's face reddened. "Then why don't you just TELL me instead of beating around the same bush? Have a little courage and spit out the words, Olivia."

Olivia shook her head, then reached across the table and snatched Tina's half-finished beer. Olivia drank it down without stopping, then shoved the empty glass back at Tina. The glass tipped over, then spun in a short arc on the table, leaving a thin line of beer in its wake.

"Courage. Bullshit, Sarah. You don't know what courage is. You think you could have had the courage to go through what I did? To live in captivity like I did? You think you'd have the courage to eat food with dirt in it? Or drink water you didn't know the source of? Would you have had the courage to live for six weeks without toilet paper or television, or LIGHTS?"

Michelle put her hand on Olivia's shoulder. "Come on, Olivia. We get it. You went through something we'll never understand. But that doesn't mean we're not all here to help you through whatever you're dealing with now."

"I shouldn't have had to go through anything. It was supposed to be Sarah," Olivia said.

"Wait, what?" Heather said.

"Yes. Her." Olivia pointed at Sarah. "Want to learn what I found out when they literally chained me up in a dirty kitchen? Susie told me she lived with her aunt right across the street from sweet little Sarah. That's what she called you. She said she tried to talk to you once, and you completely ignored her. For some reason, she became obsessed with you."

"I've never met a Susie," Sarah said.

"Doesn't matter," Olivia said with a wave of her hand. "Susie probably isn't even her real name. But, somehow, she knew you. Or thought she did. And in her maniacal brain, you did something to slight her. And that night, when we met for Cinco de Mayo? She followed you, Sarah. You. You were the target, not me. I was just the one who felt the need to step out for a breath of fresh air."

Olivia glanced around at the rest of the women at the table. No one else spoke or moved. They all looked like statues, right down to Tina's mouth, hanging ajar. Olivia reached across the table for Heather's glass, and no one tried to stop her as she drained the beer.

"I'm done here," Olivia said.

Olivia slid out of the chair and stumbled when she touched the floor. She spun around, took two steps backward, and bumped into the waitress right behind her. That caused the waitress to drop a full pitcher of beer on the patrons at the table she was serving. She also lost the beer glasses that fell and shattered as they hit the floor. The waitress pivoted to see who had hit her and pushed Olivia. Olivia, already off balance, spun, tripped on a chair leg, and fell into Sarah. Sarah's chair tipped, almost righted itself, then toppled over, sending Sarah backward onto the floor with Olivia right on top of her, nose to nose.

"Sarah?" Olivia said.

She didn't answer. Her eyes fluttered but didn't open.

"Sarah?"

Olivia shook Sarah's shoulder, but she didn't respond.

"I'm sorry. So sorry," Olivia said. She kissed Sarah gently on the lips, then stumbled to her feet. Tina and Michelle stepped in to help Sarah, but neither said a word to Olivia.

Olivia looked around for comfort in the faces of her friends, but finding none, stumbled away from the table to the door, and out into the dark night.

CHAPTER FIFTEEN

Detective Torres dropped a white bag on her guest chair. The room was warmer than usual, so she took off her coat and hung it on a hook on the inside of her office door. Since she knew the thermostat within reach didn't control a thing, she didn't attempt to adjust the temperature. She sat at her desk and shuffled through the few handwritten notes scattered on her desk while she waited for her computer to boot up. The message light on her desk phone blinked like an angry firefly, and she suspected once she dug into her email, she'd find a bunch of messages in there, too.

She heard knuckles rap on her door, and she looked up and caught Officer Press standing there, his uniform as crisp as ever.

"Yes?"

"Sorry to bother you, Detective. The chief wanted me to come by and remind you about the briefing at ten. He said he sent you several messages about it, but you never responded to any of them. I'm supposed to wait here until you give me a confirmation."

Torres sighed. "Email. Voice mail. Text messages." She

grabbed a couple of the written notes and shook them in the air for effect. "Written notes, and now we're back to messenger boys. Sorry, messenger men. I'll bet they never told you at the academy that ninety percent of detective work involved wading through correspondence, most of which are duplicated by people like the chief who can't wait ten minutes for an answer."

"No, Detective," Press said. "They never mentioned that at the academy."

"Tell the chief I'll be there at ten. You're dismissed."

"Thank you, Detective."

Press stepped from the door, but Torres stopped him by shouting his name. He stepped backward until he stood in front of her door.

"Yes, Detective?"

"Great job at the golf course the other day. Keep up the good work."

Press broke into a grin. "Thank you, Detective. I will."

Torres returned her attention to her computer and brought up the email. The machine told her she had just over four-hundred unread messages, so she clicked a button to bring up only the ones marked urgent. That brought the number down to twenty, and she noticed six of those came from the chief's office and concerned the briefing at ten. She looked at the clock and figured she had almost two full hours to prepare the presentation that was almost an exact duplicate of the presentation she'd made every day since they determined they were dealing with a serial killer.

Rather than pick up the phone and call the medical examiner's office, she picked up the white bag from the chair and headed for the elevator.

When she got to the office door with Dr. James Seer on the nameplate, she knocked on the door twice out of professional courtesy and opened it. The office looked empty, but she could tell James was in the building somewhere. His laptop was open on his desk, and his favorite leather jacket was hanging neatly on a free-standing coat rack near the door. Torres stepped in and placed the bag on his desk next to his computer, and left the room, closing the door behind her.

From Seer's office, she walked down the corridor, then pushed her way through a set of swinging doors. The look of the space changed. She'd left an area with carpet and wood doors and stepped into an area with a more clinical demeanor. The floor, bare concrete. The walls, tiled. Even the lights had changed from soft sconces in the hallway to industrial fluorescents.

The city didn't have a large budget for the office but had enough to keep two autopsy rooms and a mortuary cooler large enough to hold twelve bodies. The lights in the first autopsy room were out, so Torres moved to the second. It had a small rectangular window in the door, and when Torres peeked in, she saw Dr. Seer and an assistant performing an autopsy.

Torres opened the door without knocking, stepped into the room, and let the door auto-close behind her. Since she didn't have on any medical gear, she leaned against the wall next to the door.

"The distinguished Detective Torres," Dr. Seer said, looking up from the body. He had a scalpel in hand and placed it on a tray. The doctor was in a blue body suit and a helmet with a face shield connected to a respirator pack on his back. He stepped around the table and took a couple of steps toward her. "What can I do for you?"

"Is that the Lana Peterson case?" Torres asked, gesturing toward the body.

"No. We finished her up late yesterday. You shouldn't be in here without the proper gear. Can you go back and wait for me in my office, or I can call you at yours when I'm done here?"

"How long will you be?"

"Fifteen minutes or so."

Torres nodded. "I'll wait down here. See you in a few."

Without waiting for an answer. Torres pulled the door open and made her way back to Seer's office. She made herself comfortable behind his desk and pulled out her phone. While she waited, she ran through her email, deleting whatever she could, filing what she needed, and ignoring anything that required any proper attention on her part.

Twenty minutes later, Seer entered his office, looking dapper in green surgical scrubs. Seeing Torres in his favorite chair, he slid into the guest chair instead.

"What can I help you with, Gloria?" he asked. He spotted the bag. "Is that from Zander's?"

She pushed the bag toward him. "Yes, it is. I figured one good donut deserves another, so enjoy."

Seer opened the bag and glanced in. "There's only one in here. Where's yours?"

Torres shrugged. "I ate mine on the drive to the office. Couldn't resist, you know. So, spill it. What did you find on Lana Peterson?"

Seer pulled the donut from the bag. "Chocolate donut with chocolate frosting? Daring."

"It also has a chocolate filling. Get on with it already. What do you have?"

Seer took a large bite. The filling inside the remaining donut sagged and threatened to drop on his shirt, but a single lick held it at bay.

"What we're looking at here is a crime of opportunity, I believe."

Torres smiled. "You understand detecting is my job, right? What does the body tell you?"

"It tells me we were correct with the original assessment. The cause of death was a blow to the head. Well, several, if you want to get specific. X-rays tell me she suffered three good whacks against the wall. Possibly as many as five."

"Is whacks a medical term, Doctor?" Torres teased.

Seer swallowed another bite of the donut. "I like to make things easier for the common layperson."

"You realize I can layperson your ass right onto your own autopsy table, right, Jimmy?"

"Come on, Glory. I'm just messing with you. I did the examination and found no puncture wound as with the other four victims. For the sake of due diligence, I submitted blood and tissue samples, but I suspect she's going to come up clean. Or relatively clean, considering she was in a recovery program. I can say with certainty there won't be an overdose level of Clonazepam in her system. So far as I could tell, other than the cranial injury, Lana Peterson was in perfect health."

"No indication she swallowed the balloon?" Torres asked.

"Nope. It never got near her throat. I picked it right off her tongue."

Torres looked Seer in the eyes. "Looks to me like it was a crime of opportunity. She got pulled out the window, just like I observed on the video, and got her head smashed in the process. No chance it was an accident?"

Seer shook his head. "No. I might expect one fracture if it was an accident. Maybe two if she hit her head on the brick wall of the house and then a concrete sidewalk, but not five from that height."

"Could a woman have done this?" Torres asked.

"You still thinking the Branch woman as a suspect? Well, I can't rule her out. It wouldn't take much force to shove a head into a wall. And if the first blow stunned the victim, each subsequent blow would be that much easier."

"Okay. Thanks," Torres said as she stood. "Enjoy the donut but wipe the chocolate off your nose before you run into anyone."

"No. Wait. There's more." Seer said. He finished the donut, then reached into the bag for napkins, which he used to wipe his fingers and face.

"What?"

"The balloon. Something else that told me this wasn't a planned thing."

Torres settled back into the chair. "Go on."

"There was something about the balloon that didn't look quite right to me."

Seer leaned forward and snatched his laptop from the desk. He took a few minutes to dig through the files to find what he wanted, then put two images on a split screen. He spun the laptop around and set it down on the desk in front of Torres.

"What do you notice?"

Torres took a minute to study the images and shifted her head from one to the other like she was looking at one of those 'spot the differences' illustrations.

"The handwriting is different," Torres said at last.

"No. I believe the same hand wrote both of these messages. The one on the left, victim number four, got written in nice, straight block letters. The other balloon looks slanted, rushed. No time for neatness. Advance the screen."

Torres pushed a button and got another set of side-by-side images. On the left was a screen of red and nothing else. On the right was a large water droplet on a screen of red.

"What's this?"

"A photo taken of the inside of the balloons. The left, again, is victim four. There's nothing inside. I suspect when it got inflated, the perp did it with a little hand pump like the clowns who make balloon animals use. Smart, really, especially if you're going to inflate a balloon in someone's throat."

"And the picture on the right?"

"The perp had to inflate it in a hurry to get it big enough to write on, so they blew it up themselves. That water droplet you're looking at is spit. And do you know what we can get from spit?"

Torres sat up straighter and her eyes brightened. "DNA. Did you extract enough to do analysis on?"

"I don't know, but what I got is already at the lab. Should

have preliminary results sometime after lunch. At the least, we should be able to nail the perp down to a specific gender."

Torres picked her phone up from the desk and read the high-priority text message she'd just received. A second later, Seer's desk phone rang, and he leaned over and answered the call. He listened for a moment, asked one question, then hung up.

"Let me guess," Torres said. "You're headed over to Madison Park."

Seer stood and reached for his jacket. "No rest for the wicked. Or is it no rest for the weary? Either way, we're headed for the park."

Since Torres needed to head upstairs to her office and collect a few things before she left, Dr. Seer beat her to the crime scene.

Fifteen minutes after the doctor arrived, Torres pulled up to the curb and spotted Seer standing in front of a bench. On the bench, Torres saw someone sitting straight up, head slouched forward. She headed for the site, then did a wide arc around it when Seer waved her off.

"Watch your step. It's a mess on this side," Seer warned.

Torres took care and soon stood next to the doctor.

"I don't think this was an accident, either," Torres said.

The woman perched on the bench had her legs slightly spread, knees locked. Her arms lay at her sides, palms up. Although she leaned back on the bench, her chin touched her chest. She wore blue jeans and a white blouse. The stain on the blouse's front and the top of her jeans had dried into a deep maroon from the blood that erupted from her slashed throat.

"I hate these," Seer admitted. "Always so messy. Can you help me lay down this tarp?"

Without bothering to answer, Torres took two corners of the five-foot-square tarp. They spread it as wide as possible, then approached the bench and laid the tarp so the ends touched the bench legs. With the ground in front of the victim covered, Seer approached the body and took several photographs.

"I'm going to go out on a limb and say the victim died of exsanguination caused by a throat laceration. Looks deep. I can't say until the autopsy, but I'd guess the perp sliced both the carotid and jugular. She would have bled out pretty quickly."

"Can you guess the time of death?" Torres asked.

"There's a regular patrol at this park that runs every night until two, and it wasn't called in until this morning, so I'd guess sometime in that time frame."

"Can we move her to see if there's any ID?" Torres asked.

"Not for a bit. She's got a phone under her left hand. Let's go for that."

Seer took a couple of close-up shots of the area, then slid the phone out from under her hand, bagged it, and handed it to Torres. The phone was inside a fold-over case. She opened the case and saw the first item in there was a driver's license. "Ophelia Stein. Age twenty-three. Lives about two miles from here."

"Ophelia? That's an old name for a young woman."

Torres shrugged. "Maybe Shakespeare's making a comeback."

"She's got a couple of credit cards and some cash in here. Doesn't seem to be a robbery."

Torres fiddled with the phone. The home screen came up immediately. "Got lucky. It's unlocked."

She went right to the text messages when she saw the phone had thirty unread messages.

"This is interesting. It seems Ophelia had a falling out with a guy named Carlos yesterday. They were supposed to meet for drinks, but he bailed on her to be with his buddies."

"Oh oh. How did that turn out?" Seer asked.

"Looks like she visited the bar, anyway. She sent him a bunch of photos. Oh. Shit."

"What is it?" Seer asked.

"She's got a bunch of selfies in here. Look at this one."

Torres held the phone up so the doctor could see it. "Yeah, and?"

"And the woman in the blue sweatshirt with her arm around Ophelia looking like they're best friends is my number one suspect, Olivia Branch."

"No way. How did she go from off the grid to a party girl? Or were those from before?"

"Nope. Last night. Olivia was with this victim last night."

"You don't suppose…"

Dr. Seer didn't finish the sentence. Instead, he gently lifted the victim's head with one hand, and with the other coaxed the jaw open. "Aw, no. Get the forceps and take that out, will you?"

Torres grabbed the tool, and Seer held the mouth open while she extracted a red balloon from Ophelia's mouth.

Before dropping it into a bag, Torres stretched it out. "I'm coming for you. With a capital O."

"O for Ophelia," Seer said. "I can't believe they knew each other."

Torres went into the phone and scanned through the pictures from the previous night. "They're together in a dozen pictures. Look at this one."

She held up the phone and Seer saw the photo of the two women sharing a kiss on the lips.

"Seems like they know each other quite well," Seer said.

Torres did a little more digging into the phone's contacts. "Her number isn't listed in here that I can tell."

"Under a different name, perhaps?" Seer said.

"Doubtful. I think it's more likely they met last night. What time do you think Fig's opens?"

"Eleven," Seer said without hesitation.

"How did you know that off the top of your head?"

Seer turned around and pointed off in the distance. "I used to play in a basketball league on Saturday mornings. We'd typically finish up around eleven-thirty, then go over to Fig's for beer since it's the bar closest to here."

Torres checked the time. "I've got a couple hours then. Why don't you do what you need to do here, and I'll go make a couple of calls I really don't want to make."

"To who?" Seer asked.

"My chief, and this girl's poor parents."

CHAPTER SIXTEEN

At one, Torres parked her car outside of Fig's Bar right behind a beer truck. She left enough room for the delivery man to access the ramp behind his truck. That put her half in a delivery zone, and half in a bus stop, but at the moment, Torres cared little for proper parking regulations. From the seat next to her, she grabbed a file folder and left the car without bothering to lock the doors.

She stepped into the building and headed directly to the bar. There was already a patron sitting there watching a game show on the television above the bar while nursing a Bloody Mary with a beer chaser.

"Detective Torres," she said, showing the bartender her shield. "Can you tell me who closed last night?"

"I think it was Bernie," the bartender said. "It usually is on Sunday nights."

"Can I talk to him?" Torres asked.

"Bernie's a Bernadette. You can talk to her, but if she's working tonight, she won't be in for another six hours."

"Fine. Is your manager in yet?"

The bartender pointed toward the restrooms. "Take the stairs at the end of the hall. The owner's office is on the second floor."

Torres trudged through the bar, surprised her shoes didn't stick to the wood floor like with the establishments closer to the university downtown. She passed the restrooms and climbed the stairs at the end of the hall as instructed. At the top landing, she came to a door which was wide open. When she stepped in, she spotted the delivery man going over invoices with the bar owner.

"Sit down, Honey, I'll be right with you," the owner said.

Torres glanced off to the side and took the least broken-down looking chair of the three and waited for the men to conclude their business. When they did, the delivery man left, tipping his hat to Torres as he passed her. She smiled and nodded in return.

"Okay, Honey, come on over."

Torres stepped to the desk. "Are you Fig?" she asked.

"Technically, I'm Fig the Fourth. My great-granddaddy built this place a month after they repealed prohibition. Been in the family ever since. Are you here about the about the bar keeping job, Honey?" Fig the Fourth asked.

Torres opened her credentials. "Actually, the name is Detective Gloria Torres, not Honey. And I'm here about a murder, not a job."

"Murder? There wasn't any murder here."

"Not on premises, but I have reason to suspect that the victim was in this establishment last night. Do you mind if I show you a few pictures?"

Without waiting for an answer, Torres opened the file folder and held up a blown-up photo of Ophelia Stein. "Do you recognize her?"

"Opie? Sure. She comes in here all the time. Sometimes with her boyfriend, sometimes with her girlfriends."

"You know the boyfriend's name?"

"Carmine, I think?"

"Carlos?"

Fig snapped his fingers. "That's it. Carlos."

"Was he in here last night?"

Fig shook his head. "Couldn't tell you. I'm usually here all night on Sundays, but yesterday I wasn't feeling well, so I left around eight."

"And Bernie closed the bar?"

Fig nodded.

"I'd like her phone number and address. I need her to look through some photographs to see if she recognizes any of the people in them."

"Can I see them?"

Torres passed Fig the pictures, and he looked through them carefully.

"We don't need to wake Bernie yet. I've got a fully robust security system in here. Step into my other office."

Fig got up and walked to the side of the room where he had another desk set up. On it, he had three monitors and a wireless keyboard. Beneath the desk was a computer, and from there ran a bunch of wires to a server stack.

"Impressive setup, especially for a bar," Torres said.

"Have almost every inch of the place covered, except the bathrooms, of course. I paid almost eight grand for it back in the day."

"Seems like an expensive outlay."

"I had a bar manager skimming from the till for probably two years before I suspected him, and once I put in this system, it finally caught him. It's also reduced inventory theft, so I no longer have any thousand-dollar bottles of booze walking out the door under someone's coat. Even helped me out of a negligence case once. A lady slipped and fell and wanted to sue the pants off of me. Once I brought the video evidence before the judge of her deliberately spilling her drink to slip on, that case got tossed out of court in a hurry, and she even got fined for filing a false report or something. Anyway, yeah, it was a big initial outlay of cash, but it's already paid for itself twice over. Hand me those photos again."

Detective Torres passed him the photos.

"Can you tell me what time she took these?" Fig asked.

"The time stamp is on the back of the pictures."

Fig skipped the first picture, since it was just a copy of Ophelia's driver's license. He checked the time on the next one on the pile and brought up the security footage for the time in question. He played the file, and on screen, Ophelia came to life. She walked through the crowd like she owned the place. She stopped at the bar, ordered a shot and a beer, downed the shot, and took the beer with her as she made her rounds, taking photos with people and talking.

"Do you mind if I drive?" Detective Torres asked.

"Sure thing."

Fig left the chair and let Torres take his seat and then showed her how to use the controls to move backward and forward in time or jump to different times.

Detective Torres got a feel for the machine, then fast-forwarded her way through the footage until she found the spot where Olivia had entered the picture. As it turned out, Ophelia took the lead and brought Olivia into her circle. Once they connected, they never parted. She watched as Olivia downed drink after drink, and although there wasn't any audio in the feed, Torres could tell by the gestures and staggering that Olivia was well past drunk.

She followed the pair around the bar as they made their rounds. After an hour at the bar, Olivia went into the bathroom. A few minutes later, Olivia exited the bathroom and made a beeline for the door. A half-hour later, the bartender announced last call, and Ophelia walked out.

"Good riddance that other woman left. Was she involved? I

wouldn't be surprised."

Torres turned around. "What do you mean?"

"That girl in the blue was in earlier and caused a bit of a ruckus. Hold on."

Fig went back to his desk, rummaged around for something, and returned with a note with a date and time on it. He swapped spots with Torres, then brought up the footage and let it run. Torres watched as Olivia entered the bar, sat with her friends for a few minutes, made a scene, then stomped out.

"Wait, can you back that up?" Torres said.

Fig reversed the footage, then played it through again.

"Stop the screen, right there!"

Fig froze the frame, and Torres snapped a picture of the screen with her phone.

"Okay, now can you go to closing time last night?"

Fig did as requested, then froze at the moment Torres requested. She took another photo with her phone.

"Thanks for everything. This has been helpful," Torres said.

Twenty minutes later, Torres was back in her office. She'd barely made her seat warm when Officer Press rapped on her door and entered.

"I hate to say anything, Detective, but the chief wanted me to come get you the second you showed up."

"Let me guess, she's a little upset I missed the briefing this morning?"

The officer blushed. "A little upset would be an understatement. She used words in ways I've never heard before, and I was in the Navy for five years."

"All right. I need to get a little information together, and then I'll be right there," Torres said.

"Sorry, Detective. She gave me two choices. Bring you directly to her office or look for another job."

"Okay, okay. I got it. Did she give you a timeline?" Torres asked.

"Well, no. She just told me to bring you as soon as you got in."

"Fine. I got here fifteen minutes from now. Take a seat and wait."

Officer Press slid into the guest chair while Torres gathered her files, printed a few more pages from her laptop, and downloaded and printed the pictures she took with her phone. She took a moment to page through all the information in her folder to make sure she had everything, then headed for the door. Torres stopped and turned around. "Are you coming with me, Officer?"

Press jumped to his feet and followed Torres to the elevator. Eventually, the car came and took them two floors higher. Officer Press took the lead and ushered the detective into the chief's office. They briefly paused at the receptionist's desk, but he just pointed to the inner office and the duo kept walking.

Chief Sonya Roberts stood just inside her door and let Detective Torres in. She stepped in front of Officer Press and blocked his entry.

"Thank you, Officer, you're dismissed," the chief said, closing the door before she finished her sentence.

Although Chief Roberts stood a good three inches shorter than Detective Torres, she more than made up for the height difference with attitude and authority. Rumor around the office was that the chief was half Irish and half honey badger. Like Officer Press, the chief always wore her uniform, and her Caesar cut silver hair implied she meant all business. Roberts stepped around her desk and sat. Torres didn't bother to look for a seat since she knew there were no other chairs in the room.

"Update. Go," Roberts demanded.

Detective Torres did her best to make a concise update of the six cases, including her coordination with the medical examiner's office. As she discussed each victim, she presented the pictures as evidence. Roberts sat cross-armed and stone-faced through the entire presentation and didn't say a word until Torres finished.

"What's the update on the Branch woman? I understand you found a bunch of evidence at her home?"

"We've been unable to track her down. I have a unit posted at her home, but she hasn't turned up there."
Roberts picked up the photos and shuffled through them. "Isn't this her?"

Torres looked at the photo in the chief's outstretched hand. "Yes."

"You're telling me that the entire police department of this city can't track down one person who appears to be drunk most of the time? Obviously, she's staying in the area. Find her, Torres. Serve your warrant and arrest her. If she's not downstairs in booking by sundown, you'll be out on the street yourself. Got it?"

"Yes, Chief."

Roberts handed Torres her files, and Torres left the office. She'd made it all the way to the elevator when the folder slid from her grasp, cascading the photos onto the floor.

"Crap," Torres said.

She bent over to scoop them up, and as she did, something caught her eye. Torres shuffled through the pictures, sorting them in descending order according to death date, then read the message as she saw it.

"Olivia, I'm coming for you. Oh, crap." Torres swept up the photos, forgot about the elevator, and ran for the stairs.

* * *

Detective Torres arrived at Olivia's apartment building in a marked patrol car, lights flashing and sirens blaring. When she pulled up, the front tire rolled up on the curb, but she thought nothing of it as she shut down the car and ran into the building. Without hesitation, she jogged up the stairs and down the hallway.

Outside Olivia's door, an officer stood at his post. Torres didn't recognize him, so she flashed his credentials in his face and beat hard on the door loud enough for the entire building to hear.

A few seconds later, the door swung open, and Torres stepped in without waiting to be invited.

"We need to find Olivia," Torres said, coming right to the point. "If you have any idea of where she is, you need to tell me. Now."

"I don't know where she is. You can check the apartment if you like. I came by to see if she was here and to feed Nibbler."

"Stay here," Torres said.

The detective sped through and did a quick check of the apartment and determined Heather was telling the truth.

"Do you know where your friend is?" Torres said.

"I told you. I have zero clue. It's been a couple of days since I've seen her," Heather said.

"Bullshit. You saw her last night down at Fig's Bar. She came in while you were there with your friends, made a scene, assaulted a waitress, and left."

"How did you know that?" Heather asked.

"I've got you all on video. I also have Olivia returning to that bar a few hours later and hanging out with a woman who ended up dead this morning."

Heather didn't respond.

"Look, Heather, Olivia's not in any trouble. But I need to find her. Immediately. She's in danger. Do any of your group live near here? Someone she'd go bunk with?"

Heather shook her head. "The only one who lives close by is Sarah, and Olivia won't go there."

"How did she even know to show up at that bar last night?"

"I've been wondering that myself," Heather said. "The only way she could have found out about it is…" Heather slapped her forehead. "The group chat. She's a part of that group."

"Can I read the messages?" Torres asked.

Heather retrieved her phone from the island, unlocked it, opened the app, and handed it over.

Torres quickly scrolled through the messages. "It's no wonder she showed up angry. In her state, she probably thought you were pulling one over on her."

Heather dropped her head. "I guess she could have taken it that way, but that's not the way we meant it."

"Can you think of where she might go?" Torres asked.

"No, but. Wait. I almost forgot. I installed a tracking app on her phone when I thought she might sneak out to buy alcohol."

Heather snatched back her phone and brought up the app. She looked at the screen and smiled. "I know where she is."

"Good. You're coming with me. I'm afraid she'll run if she sees me."

"Okay. Let's go."

Torres parked a half block from the laundromat and let Heather out. Heather walked to the door and looked in before entering. Off in the back corner, she spotted Olivia sitting in a chair, head back, obviously asleep.

Heather waved for Torres to join her, then entered the laundromat. She thought of sneaking up on Olivia, but the closer she got, the more she realized Olivia was totally out of it. When Heather spotted the two empty vodka bottles at Olivia's feet, she realized why.

Heather heard something behind her, turned, and saw Torres standing just inside the door. She pivoted and called Olivia's name. Olivia didn't respond, so Heather reached out and gently shook her shoulder.

Olivia moaned, but didn't respond otherwise.

Heather shook Olivia a little harder and called her name. This time, Olivia's eyes fluttered open.

"Heather?"

"Yes, Olivia. It's Heather. It's time to go. Torres, come and help me."

Torres approached the women, and each one took one of Olivia's arms and lifted her gently from the chair. Together, they half-carried, half-dragged Olivia out of the building and got her situated in the back of the police car.

Heather got in the passenger seat up front and buckled herself in. "So, where are we going?"

"Not back to either of your homes, that's for sure," Torres said. "There's a safe house on the other side of town. I think I'll set you up there for now."

"Why do we need a safe house?" Heather asked.

"Remember those murders I told you about? We've had another since then. We found the body this morning. The victim was someone Olivia met at the bar last night."

"You don't think Olivia could have killed anyone?"

"Honestly, she was my primary suspect. But I saw something else on the video from the bar. And I saw some evidence from all the crimes in a new light that tells me she's not the criminal. She's the target."

CHAPTER SEVENTEEN

Heather and Torres got Olivia undressed down to her underwear and got her into bed. They quietly left the room and sat at the four-person table in the kitchen. Torres had taken them to a residential area in the sleepy part of town. The house was a small craftsman, with only two bedrooms and one bathroom, but its unassuming character was perfect for a safe house.

"You don't have anything to worry about here. In fact, one of my officers lives only two doors down."

"Which direction?" Heather asked.

Torres cracked a smile. "Toward the school. The blue house with the white trim."

Torres got up, opened the fridge, and found it empty. She opened the cabinet next to the fridge. That she found fully stocked.

"You're in luck. Providing you like soup, and provided that soup you like is either tomato or chicken noodle. I'll have one of my officers bring by some real groceries. Either of you have any food allergies or special dietary requirements I should know about?"

"No, not really," Heather said. "How long do you think we'll be here?"

"It's hard to say, so we'll plan for a week and adjust from there. If you give me the keys to your places, I'll get you enough changes of clothes to get you through."

"Why can't I just go? I won't be gone long, and I know exactly what we need and where everything is."

"You don't seem to get it," Torres said. "There's someone after Olivia. And by extension, you may be in danger, too. It's important we keep you both off the grid until we find who is after her."

"So, what can we do?" Heather asked.

"Sit tight. Watch the television. Play cards. Read. Take naps. I don't care. Do not leave this house."

"What about Olivia? She needs help."

Torres sat silent for a moment. "She certainly can't go back to the facility. What about that therapist? If you got her to come here, perhaps she could do something for Olivia in the interim."

"I should call her. I'm worried about Olivia, especially if she's drinking herself into blackouts."

"Okay. If you can set up a home visit, I'll make sure the doctor has clearance to get in here. No one gets past the front door without my approval, so don't plan on ordering a pizza or any takeout Chinese."

"That's too bad. I really love the dim sum at Chen's," Heather said.

"If that's the case, you tell us, and we'll bring it over."

"So, we're stuck here."

"Afraid so," Torres said.

Heather exhaled and drummed her fingers on the wood tabletop. After a few unbroken minutes of silence, she reluctantly dug into the front pocket of her jeans and dropped her keys on the table. "Can you send a female officer? I don't like the idea of some strange man going through my underwear drawer."

Torres scooped up the keys. "Deal."

Torres showed Heather around the house, stopping to highlight a red phone in the living room that was hard-wired as a direct line to the police station. Once the tour was complete, Torres checked to make sure she had drawn all the shades, then left the house.

Heather moved into the second bedroom to check on Olivia, who, fortunately, was still snoring away with fervor. She left the room, closing the door behind her, and retreated to the living room. There, she turned on the television and flipped through all the channels without stopping more than a few seconds at a time to determine what the program was. When she passed through every option, she settled on a movie she'd seen a thousand times before.

She watched the show for an hour, then, realizing she hadn't eaten since breakfast, rose and wandered into the kitchen. Like Torres had done, Heather checked the fridge and rummaged through every cabinet in search of food. Finding only the soup, Heather grabbed a can of chicken noodle soup and rummaged through the cabinets again until she found a pot to warm it in. She opened the can, dumped the contents into the pot, and added a can full of water to it. She put it on the stove, set the burner on low, and searched the kitchen again for something to drink. Heather found nothing, so she grabbed a glass and settled for water from the faucet.

After drinking the water and refilling her glass, Heather returned to the cabinet and found a bowl, but when she rummaged through the silverware drawer, she couldn't find any spoons. She replaced the bowl and instead found an over-sized green coffee mug and a fork. When the soup steamed, Heather placed the mug on the counter and poured the soup from the pot, using the fork to make sure she dumped a good helping of noodles in there as well.

Heather took the mug and sat at the kitchen table. She

brought the mug to her lips, and blew at the soup four times, something she did more out of habit than out of necessity. She took a sip and leaned back in her chair.

"That smells good."

Heather turned and spotted Olivia standing outside the kitchen in her underwear, her arms wrapped around her body in a self-hug.

"Why don't you go put on your clothes and while you're gone, I'll make you a mug."

Olivia gave a demure nod and padded down the hallway. Once she turned into the bedroom, Heather rose, fished out another coffee mug, this one the color of a marigold, and poured the remains of the pot into the mug, then set it at the table. She sat, then rose and retrieved a fork for Olivia.

While she waited for Olivia to return, Heather sipped at her soup. Eventually, Olivia returned and slid into a chair.

Olivia lifted the mug, and without checking the temperature, drank.

"This is good," she said, setting the mug on the table. "I can't remember the last time I had plain old chicken noodle soup." Olivia had a little more broth and scooped some noodles into her mouth using the fork. She chewed, swallowed, and reached for Heather's water.

Heather pushed the glass across the table and got up for a second glass. Olivia drank, then turned her attention back to the soup. After a few more bites, she pushed the mug aside.

"Heather?"

"Yea?" Heather said, returning to her seat.

"Where are we, and why are we here?"

"You don't remember?"

Olivia shook her head.

"What's the last thing you do remember?"

Olivia stared at the table for a while, as if tracing the contours of the wood with her eyes would somehow kick-start her recollections. "I have no idea."

"Okay. Let's go backward. Do you remember us picking you up at the laundromat earlier today?"

Olivia shook her head.

"Do you remember coming and making a scene at Fig's Bar last night?"

Olivia hesitated, then shook.

"Oh, Liv. Okay. The long and short of it is you're in a police safe house."

"Why? Did I get arrested?"

"No. Detective Torres brought us here for protection. She's convinced there's someone after you."

Olivia's eyes widened as the color drained from her skin. She pushed back from the table, chair legs screeching across the linoleum floor.

"It's Susie, isn't it! I need to get out of here!"

"No, wait!" Heather yelled. She reached out to grab Olivia by the arm, but Olivia had already sprinted from the kitchen and was in a full run to the door.

Olivia threw open the door and ran out of the house. Not knowing where she was, she stopped in the middle of the sidewalk and looked around. Across the street, she saw a man step out of a sedan and start jogging her way.

Olivia spun around as Heather got to her and rushed right into Heather's arms. Heather took Olivia into her chest and wrapped her arms around her and held her.

"It's okay, Liv."

"You need help here, ma'am?" the man asked as he got to them.

"No, officer. She just got a little spooked. We're fine. Aren't we, Olivia?"

"Okay. You should move back into the house, please. You need to limit your outdoor time. If you need something, call us on the red phone."

"Okay. Thank you. You know what? There are no spoons in the house. Or anything to drink other than tap water."

"I'll take care of it. Go on, now."

"Come on, Liv, we need to move back into the house, okay?" Heather said.

Heather began taking baby steps backward, and since she didn't release the hug, Olivia had to go with her. After a few feet, she broke the embrace, grabbed Olivia's hand, and guided her toward the door. Heather coaxed Olivia inside the house and turned back and waved at the officer.

"Thanks, again."

Heather watched as the officer headed back to his car, then stepped into the living room and closed and locked the door behind her.

"Liv, we can't run out like that."

"Who was that man?" Olivia jabbed at the air toward the door.

"A policeman. There will always be police watching us. For our safety," Heather said. With each sentence, she softened her tone, hoping to calm her friend. "Come on, let's go sit on the couch and watch TV."

Without waiting for a response, Heather guided Olivia to the couch and sat her down. She handed Liv the remote and as she scrolled; Heather retrieved her phone.

"Olivia, I know you're stressed out. Can I call Dr. Longstreet and see if she could come over and talk to you?"

"We can't go there?"

"No. We can't go anywhere. But Detective Torres said the doctor can come to visit you. Would that be all right?"

Olivia nodded, so Heather left her watching a game show and trotted off to the bedroom to make the call. When she returned twenty minutes later, Olivia had fully extended on the couch, hand out, remote on the floor. Heather headed to the bedroom, retrieved a blanket, covered up Liv, then worked on cleaning up the soup dishes in the kitchen.

She'd just finished hand washing the pot when she heard a knock at the door. Heather glanced over at the couch, saw Liv hadn't moved, and rushed to answer. She looked through the peephole and saw two officers in uniform. She opened the door and moved so they could get in.

The woman officer carried two duffel bags. The teal one Heather recognized as her own, the purple one she assumed belonged to Olivia.

"Here are some things," the officer said, placing the bags in the living room. She handed a business card to Heather. "My number at the station. I've jotted my cell number on the back if you need anything. Oh, your keys." She rummaged in her coat pocket, found what she needed, and placed Heather's keys on the table.

"I forgot to mention Nibbler," Heather said.

"That cute mouse? I fed and watered him before I left. I'll check on him again in a couple of days."

While Heather chatted with the woman, the man unloaded the grocery bags and filled the fridge and empty cabinet. Heather saw him slide a box of plastic forks, knives, and spoons on the table. Without a word, he finished his job and left the house, followed by his partner.

Heather opened the fridge and saw a lot more options. She spotted a package of ground beef, four chicken breasts, a half-gallon of milk, a variety of fruits and vegetables. Along with containers of orange and grape juice, a couple of two-liters of Coca-Cola, and a six-pack of beer. The beer she removed from the fridge, took it outside, called the on-duty officer over, and handed it to him.

When she returned to the kitchen, she found Olivia at the table eating a fun-sized chocolate bar.

"Where did you get that?" Heather asked.

Olivia pointed. "The empty cabinet is magic. There's

chocolate there now."

Heather smiled and searched for a piece for herself. She found the chocolate, pulled two bottles of water from a case the officer dropped off, and handed one to Olivia.

"How are you doing?" Heather asked.

"I'm tired and I have a headache. I could drink a gallon of water. The lights in here are all too bright."

"So, you're hungover. I'm not surprised."

"Did you get a hold of the doctor?" Olivia asked.

"Yes. She'll be here sometime tomorrow. She has a client at eight, so we should expect her around nine-thirty."

Olivia nodded, got up, and headed for the cabinet for another chocolate.

"Bring the bag," Heather said.

The pair polished off half of the bag before Olivia yawned. "I think I'm headed for bed."

Without waiting for a response, she rose and left the table, only to return and grab her water bottle.

"Night," Olivia said.

Heather watched her leave, then took a lap around the living room and kitchen. She turned off the television and straightened the couch's throw pillows before returning to the kitchen, where she gathered up the chocolate wrappers and tossed them in the trash. She shut off the lights and retired to her bedroom. Heather took a shower and got into bed.

* * *

Olivia woke with a start and propped herself up on one elbow.

"Heather? Is that you?" Olivia asked.

Liv strained to hear the sound that had woken her, but it didn't repeat. She put her feet on the floor and checked her phone. According to the display, it was a few minutes after three in the morning. She remembered turning her bedroom light on before going to bed, but it was now off. The room stayed fairly bright thanks to the bathroom light.

Olivia got out of bed and plodded to the bathroom. Although the light stung her eyes, she was grateful Heather left it on. She did her business and took a moment to wash her hands and splash her face. Liv looked in the mirror and didn't recognize the red, dry eyes looking back at her. She washed her face a second time, dried herself off, and left the bathroom, leaving the light on behind her.

She crept to Heather's room. The door was only open a crack, so Olivia opened it wider until the light from the bathroom spilled over Heather's bed. Olivia wanted to get into bed with her, but Heather lay on her stomach, her arms and legs splayed out, so she looked like a giant letter X. Since Heather had only a twin-sized bed, Olivia realized she'd need to be a cat to get in there to snuggle with her.

Instead, Olivia closed the door and moved back to her own room.

She'd made it almost to her bed when someone grabbed her from behind, wrapped a gloved hand around her mouth, then pushed her forward. Olivia landed face down on her bed, the breath knocked from her body, the added weight crushing her into the mattress.

She tried to scream but couldn't with her mouth covered. She breathed in, tasted earth, as if the glove had recently worked in peat moss, and choked.

"Do you remember me, Olivia?" a voice whispered in her ear. "Do you remember the games we played?"

Olivia struggled, attempting to break free, but couldn't. She tried to scream again, but got out nothing more than a squeak, much like the ones Nibbler gave every time Olivia came into view.

"I can't tell you how excited I am to play the game again,"

the voice said.

To Olivia, the voice sounded eerily calm, detached. The coldness in the tone froze her blood. She shook her body and managed to free one leg. Olivia kicked backward, catching the person in their back.

The hand went from covering her mouth to grabbing her hair. They jerked her head back, giving Olivia just enough time to inhale a fresh breath of air before slamming her back down and pushing her face deeper into the pillow.

"You shouldn't do that," the voice whispered in Olivia's ear. It was close enough she could feel the vile warmth of their breath and a stench that reminded her of sour milk.

On instinct, Olivia inhaled, but found no oxygen, but instead only the strange taste of the laundered pillowcase. She squirmed again, then tried to redouble her effort when her attacker pawed at her pajama bottoms. She tried to grind her hips into the bed, but the hands were too overpowering, and she soon felt the cool night air on her buttocks.

Her mind raced to the worst of humiliations.

A second later, she got a pinch in her left buttock, then a stinging sensation.

Once again, they pulled her hair to lift her head, and Olivia took large gulps of air before being pushed back into the pillow.

"That's all for tonight. I'll see you soon," the voice said.

The pressure left Olivia's body, and she heard a door open. She rolled over and placed her feet flat on the floor. Liv reached an arm out to the door and tried to call for Heather, but her voice wouldn't work. She took a step toward the door, felt dizzy, and collapsed.

CHAPTER EIGHTEEN

Heather moaned and rolled over in bed. She groaned and managed to sit up. Her hands moved to her temples, which pounded like waves against a breakwater.

"Oh, Heather, what did you do last night?"

Heather used the bed as support to get to her feet and swayed as she walked to the door. She stopped for a moment to brace herself against the doorjamb, then headed for the bathroom. The second her feet hit the tiled floor, Heather felt nauseous. She had barely lifted the lid when she emptied the contents of her stomach into the bowl. After the worst had passed, she leaned on the sink for support as she watched the remnants of the previous night's snack swirl below her.

"Must be bad chocolate," she said as she flushed the toilet.

After using the facilities for their intended purpose, Heather opened a drawer and discovered a fresh toothbrush, used it, and washed her face. Feeling better, she returned to her room, got dressed, and checked her phone.

"Noon? How the hell can it be noon?"

Heather moved from her room to the common areas,

expecting to spot Olivia munching on something in the kitchen or watching TV in the living room. Olivia was in neither room, so Heather turned and headed back down the hall.

"Olivia, hey, why did…"

Heather stopped in her tracks when she spotted Olivia lying on the floor. She was on her side, and when Heather kneeled on the floor, she spotted a puddle of vomit on the carpet and a dried patch around her mouth.

"Olivia? Liv?" Heather asked, shaking Olivia's shoulder. "Olivia?" Heather's voice raised in pitch when she didn't get a response the first time. She shook Olivia harder and relaxed a bit when Olivia let out a prolonged moan.

Heather rubbed Olivia's arm and continued talking to her until she regained a state of semi-consciousness. Although Heather's rubbery legs could barely support herself, she managed to pick Olivia up from the floor and got her seated on the bed.

"Olivia, what happened?"

"What?" Olivia said. She closed her eyes again and slumped onto her pillow.

Heather retrieved a glass of water from the kitchen, roused Olivia, and held it while Olivia drank. Olivia worked her way through half a glass of water, then suddenly pushed Heather's hand away. Heather lost her grip on the glass, and it hit the wall, cracked into thirds, and dropped to the floor, leaving a trail of water on the paint.

Olivia screamed loud enough to scare Heather, and she kicked at the mattress until she backed against the headboard. Olivia brought her knees to her chest, wrapped her arms around them, and started rocking back and forth.

"She was here, Heather. She was here!"

"Who, Olivia?"

"Susie! Susie was here last night!" Olivia stopped rocking, but the tears started flowing in large drops that rolled down her cheeks and dropped to her pajama top.

"When?" Heather asked.

"Around three. I got up to go to the bathroom, and when I got back, she grabbed me! She grabbed me and threw me down on the bed and told me the game wasn't over yet! Then she pulled my pants down and stabbed me with something!"

"What? Show me," Heather said.

Olivia pushed away from the headboard, got to her feet, and dropped her drawers.

"Right here," she said, pointing to the spot.

Heather bent to get a closer look and spotted a drop of dried blood on Olivia's rump. Although she touched the spot as gently as she could, Olivia still pulled away in pain.

"Okay. Pants up. Are you okay to be here alone while I make a phone call?"

"Can you help me into the bathroom?" Olivia asked?

Heather did so, and once Olivia got settled, Heather made a beeline for the red phone. She expected it to ring somewhere when she picked it up, but instead, someone answered the line before Heather detected so much as a dial tone.

"Do you need help?" the voice said.

"Yes. We had an intruder." Heather waited for a response, then heard a pounding on the door. She hung up the phone and answered the door. When she did, two officers in uniform and one in plainclothes pushed their way in.

"I'm Corporal Camay," the plainclothes officer said, holding out his shield when he came in. "Where's the other one?" he asked.

"She's in the bathroom."

Camay nodded and addressed the officers. "Clear everything in the house except the bathroom. Look in every closet. Look under every bed. Check every space that a person could fit in. Go."

While the officers fanned out to search the house, Camay

guided Heather to the couch.

"What happened?" Camay asked.

"Olivia says she got assaulted last night by the person who kidnapped her last year. It looks like she has a needle mark on her butt, so I think she's been drugged."

"Stacy?"

"Susie."

"Did you see Susie?"

"No. I was out all night. I slept right through until noon, which is unusual for me."

"Any chance they got you, too?" Camay asked.

Heather paused. "I'll be right back."

She rushed to the bathroom and knocked on the closed door. "Olivia? It's Heather. Can you let me in?"

Olivia unlocked the door, and it cracked open. Heather slipped into the bathroom, then locked the door. She pulled off her T-shirt and dropped it on the closed toilet lid and checked her torso and arms in the mirror. Heather turned around and checked her back. She found nothing, so she dropped and stepped out of her pants and looked over the front of her legs.

"Can you check the back of my legs?" Heather asked.

"For what?" Olivia asked.

"A spot of blood, or maybe something that looks like a bug bite."

Heather spun around and Olivia gave her a once-over and shook her head. "There's nothing here."

"Hold on," Heather said.

Heather dropped her underwear to her knees. "Anything on my ass?"

Olivia gave a nervous giggle. "What I won't do for a friend."

Heather bent over and Olivia got as close as she dared. "I don't see anything."

Heather gave a half-turn.

"Wait, there it is. On your hip," Olivia said.

Heather turned so she could see herself in the mirror and rubbed at the spot. She inhaled when she touched it.

"Smarts, doesn't it?" Olivia said.

"It does. I think they hit the bone. Are you done in here? There are police officers out there."

Olivia nodded.

Heather took a moment to get dressed, and both women left the bathroom and moved into the living room.

"There's no one here but these two," an officer reported to Camay when he entered the room a minute later.

"Okay. I want one of you posted at this door, another in the backyard. If anyone without a badge approaches the house, you either arrest them or shoot them. Got it?"

The officer nodded and left the house in a hurry.

"I've contacted Detective Torres. She'll be here shortly," Camay said.

"You want us to tell you what happened?" Heather asked.

Camay checked his wristwatch and shook his head. "Let's wait for the detective. Then you won't have to repeat the story."

As Olivia settled into the chair, Heather headed into the kitchen and made two cups of coffee, added a splash of milk and a package of sugar to each mug, and gave one to Olivia. Heather joined her on the couch and made sure Olivia drank, and Heather followed her with each sip. As she drank, the fog in her head cleared, little by little.

Fifteen minutes later, the door opened, and Torres stormed in, brow creased, her heels clicking on the floor so hard they could have dented the subfloor.

"Ladies," Torres said, softening her persona as she spotted them on the couch.

Torres went to the kitchen and retrieved a chair. She set it directly before the couch, then pulled out her phone.

"I'm recording this, okay?"

Olivia and Heather both nodded.

"Good. What happened here last night?"

The women looked at each other, then Heather put her hand on Olivia's knee for encouragement.

"Go on. Tell her," Heather said.

Everyone waited patiently while Olivia finished her cup of coffee. She put the empty mug on the cushion next to her, and when it started to tip, Torres leaned over, grabbed it, and handed it to Camay.

"Any time you're ready, Olivia," Torres said.

Olivia stared into space for a few minutes, then took a deep breath and recounted her encounter with the intruder. Heather, Camay, and Torres remained silent, not interrupting as Olivia passed through the tale. As she talked, she subconsciously shifted closer to Heather, who eventually took her hand.

When she finished speaking, Olivia snuggled in closer to Heather and waited for a response.

"Can you corroborate any of her story?" Torres asked Heather.

"No. I was dead to the world. I found what I think is a needle mark on my hip, though. So, I think they injected me with whatever they got Olivia with."

"Can I see?" Torres asked.

Heather pried herself away from Olivia's grip, stood, and pulled down her sweatpants enough for the detective to examine the site.

Torres looked closely, then leaned back. "Could be a needle mark. Could be a bug bite."

"Unless there are a hive of bees in here somewhere we don't know about, I'm pretty sure it's a needle mark," Heather said, the snark apparent in her voice.

Torres stared at her for a minute. "Camay, get medical in here. I'd like them to examine the wounds, take some blood. Also, call forensics in here and get them to search the bedrooms."

"On it," Camay said. Without excusing himself, he stepped

from the room.

"Did you have anything to drink last night, Olivia?"

"No," Olivia said. "Nothing."

Torres stared at the woman, looking for facial tics or other physical indicators to tell if she was lying.

"There's nothing here to drink, detective," Heather said, defending her friend. "Your cops dropped off a six-pack of beer yesterday, but I got that out of the house as soon as I spotted it."

"What did you do with it?"

"I gave it to the cop watching the house from the car across the street."

Torres nodded. "And there was no other alcohol in the house?"

"Not a drop. With everything Olivia's been going through, I checked every inch of this place after she went to sleep yesterday."

Camay entered the house and approached the detective. "Medical and forensics are both on the way. Medical is only about five minutes out. Forensics will be about fifteen."

"Good," Torres said. "Can you answer another question for me?"

"Sure thing, Detective."

"Can you tell me how in the hell someone got in here last night?" Torres said. She said it in such a low voice, Camay had to lean in to pick up her words. Then he took a step back when he realized her infamous temper might take over.

"I don't know, Detective."

"Who was on duty last night? Doesn't matter. Find out whoever was supposed to be watching this place, then send one of the men out there to drag them out of bed and get their ass down here. Is that order clear?"

"Okay, Detective."

"Camay?"

"Yes?"

"Why are you still here?"

Camay took the hint and rushed from the house.

Torres turned her attention back to Olivia and Heather. "We're going to get you checked out, and I want to get your blood drawn to see what you got dosed with. The forensics teams will need to examine your bedrooms, so don't go back in there for now."

A knock at the door interrupted Torres. As she walked to the door, she pulled the gun from her holster. Torres checked the peephole, then secured her weapon before she opened the door.

"Torres," the paramedic said as he entered the room.

"Welling," Torres responded. "Where's your partner?"

"Out in the bus. She told me I could probably handle this on my own."

"Get to it then. I want the women in here looked over. There's an injection site on both of them, and I'd like blood drawn on each and sent to the lab for analysis. Got it?"

Welling nodded, then turned to the women. "Well, who wants to go first?" Olivia volunteered, and Welling led her into the kitchen, where he placed his gear on the table.

Torres turned her attention to Heather when her phone rang. She answered, held a terse conversation, then hung up.

"I've got to run out for a bit," Torres said to Heather. "Camay will be in here soon and will stay with you until I get back. Remember, no bedroom access until my people have cleared it."

Heather nodded her acknowledgment, and Torres left the house.

* * *

Torres pulled to the curb and parked behind a police cruiser. She got out of her car and slid into the passenger seat of the cop car.

"What did you find out, Press?"

"I found your guy," Press said. "Took me a few overtime hours and a pair of worn-out shoes, but I got him."

Press grabbed a file folder from the dashboard, opened it, and removed several photographs. "This one was the easiest to get. Your buddy Fig has quite the system."

Torres accepted the photo Press handed her. It showed a picture of Fig's Bar, taken from a camera positioned below the television above the bar. In it, Ophelia was holding a shot of liquor up as if in the middle of a toast. To her right, Olivia stood. Torres noticed her shot glass was already empty.

"Look here," Press said, using the pen to tap on the picture.

Torres did. In the photo, almost out of view, stood a man. He dressed all in black, including a black sweatshirt that appeared out of place in the warm confines of the bar. Torres noted that no one else was wearing so much as a windbreaker or a light sweater. The man wore a trucker hat, also in black, with no logo on the front. He wore it pulled low over his eyes, as if he were in centerfield trying to block out the sun.

Press took the photo from Torres and replaced it with another. This one showed the same man, this time walking down the street.

"Where's this one from?" Torres asked.

"Taken from a doorbell camera, about a block away from where Lana Peterson fell out the window." Press took that photo and replaced it with another.

Torres didn't need to ask where this photo was from. In it, she clearly saw Olivia sleeping in the back corner of the laundromat. The mysterious man in black was standing behind a row of washers watching the woman sleep.

"You got a name on this guy?" Torres asked.

"Clifford Hines. He's got a sheet. A couple of assaults. Stalking. Has a half-dozen restraining orders, and he's the lead suspect in a couple homicide cases, but those are lacking evidence, so no charges were filed yet."

"Did you get a warrant?" Torres asked. "Please tell me you did."

Press smiled. "As luck would have it, he has one outstanding. Second thing I checked."

"Good job, Press. Way to take initiative. I'm putting you in for a commendation."

"Thanks, Detective."

"All right, then. If you got the paperwork, it's time to go."

Torres and Press left the car, headed across the street, and stepped into the six-story building.

Like most buildings in the area, this one was showing its age. The concrete steps in front looked cracked and pitted, several bricks were missing from the facade, and several of the windowpanes facing the street had long cracks in them. Whatever the original color of the building had been, it took on the color of faded paint and city dust.

As they approached the building, Torres noticed a security system near the entry door, but she didn't think twice about it when she saw the door standing ajar. She opened it and stepped onto the cracked and dirty linoleum floor of the entryway. They were in the short passage with a row of mailboxes and a second security door, this one missing a doorknob completely.

Once they passed through the second door, they got a choice between walking up five flights of stairs and taking the elevator, but that choice got made for them when Torres noticed the out-of-order sign on the lift.

"I guess we're getting our steps in today," Torres said as she entered the stairwell.

Slowly, they ascended the five flights of stairs and found apartment 5A right at the top of them.

Officer Press stepped in front of the door and was about to knock when Torres grabbed his arm.

"Are you crazy? You don't stand there like that, you—"

Torres heard the sound the sound of a shotgun racking

behind the door and shoved Press hard enough to send him sprawling in the hallway. A second later, there was a loud blast, followed by an explosion of pellets and wood, when a massive hole appeared in the door where Press had stood a second before.

"Clifford Hines, this is the police. Put the gun down and come out!" Torres yelled.

Down the corridor, a door opened, and an elderly man stepped into the hallway.

"Press, get that lunatic back in his apartment!"

Press, still on the ground, turned his head and saw the man. He scrambled to his feet, rushed down the hallway, and literally shoved the man back into his apartment.

"Hines. Come out!"

"Screw you!" Hines yelled.

He racked the gun again, pulled the trigger, and expanded the size of the hole in the door, peppering the apartment door across the hall with shrapnel.

Torres grabbed her weapon, turned off the safety, and paused. She heard the gun rack, and a moment later, another shot came through the door. The second the report died, Torres pivoted, kicked in the remainder of the door, and it fell off its hinges. Hines raised the shotgun again, but before he could get it level, Torres put three bullets in his chest.

CHAPTER NINETEEN

The afternoon passed slowly for Heather and Olivia as they took their turns with the paramedic, then waited for the forensics team to come and leave. They sat on the couch for most of the time, Heather trying to read, but unable to concentrate, causing her to read the same page over until she finally grasped enough of the concept to move on to the next page. Olivia worked the remote like she was on a chemical-induced adrenaline high. She sat on the floor, cross-legged, fingering the buttons like she was playing a piano. She'd land on a channel, stay for a moment and move on. Heather watched for a while, her eyes peering over the top of the book, and noticed Olivia seemed to shy away from any program, but instead landed on commercial after commercial as if her brain would only focus on a fifteen or thirty-second snippet of information.

"Olivia," Heather said, putting the book down without bothering to place a bookmark between the pages. She'd need to start over, anyway.

"Yeah?" Olivia responded without removing her attention from the television.

"You hungry?" Heather asked.

The sun prepared to dip into the horizon, and the women hadn't had the desire to eat so much as a breadcrumb. When Heather opened the cabinet earlier, she became nauseated at the sight of the bag of chocolate, and without asking Olivia or any fanfare, she dropped it into the trash.

"I could eat," Olivia answered. She rose and joined Heather on the couch. Turning off the TV, she put the remote on the end table. "What are you up for?"

"How about some fried chicken?" Corporal Camay said from the kitchen where he was working hard on an ancient Sudoku puzzle book he'd found in a drawer.

"If you want to go, we can probably handle things on our own," Heather said.

Camay put the pen in the book to not lose his place and closed it. "Nope. The detective told me to sit with you until she returned, so that's what I'm going to do."

"Do you know when she'll get here?" Olivia asked.

"She got involved in… an incident. Those take time to work through, but I'm sure she'll be here soon. So, how about that chicken?"

Heather and Olivia looked at each other. Olivia shrugged. "Why not?"

"Great," Camay said. "What do you want for sides? French fries? Green beans? Potato salad? Coleslaw?"

"It really doesn't matter to us," Heather said.

"One of each, then. Excellent choice. I'll call it in, and it should be here within thirty minutes."

"That's quick," Heather said.

Camay chuckled. "We get expedited service. It's a long story about the restaurant owner's son and a baggie of cocaine, but I'm not supposed to talk about that."

Heather smiled. "I think you just did."

Camay glanced at her for a moment and shrugged. "Most of

the juicy details got into the papers anyway."

Heather moved from the living room to the kitchen, pulled three plates from the cabinet, and placed them on the table. Next to the plates, she added a roll of paper towels and the box of plastic cutlery. Noticing beverages were missing, she asked Olivia and Camay what they preferred to drink, and added the requested drinks to the table. Once she set the place settings to three seats, she sat at the table next to Camay.

"How long do you plan on staying?" Heather asked.

Camay took his Sudoku book and slid it to the unoccupied seat to get it out of the way. "Until Detective Torres comes to relieve me. Like I said before, I'm staying put until she gets here."

"Something I'm curious about. If she's a detective, and you're a corporal, don't you outrank her?" Heather asked.

Camay smiled. "How did you know that?"

"I dated a cop for a few months. He was obsessed with moving up the ladder and I learned more about your ranks than I wanted or needed to."

"Well, technically, you're right about that. I am one rung above Detective Torres, but because of what happened to Olivia, your friend turned into an overnight sensation across every law enforcement agency in the country. Since Torres picked up Olivia's missing persons case last year, the chief made it known that Torres is the lead on anything even remotely involving Olivia Branch. From these crazy murders right on down to if she got a ticket for littering. All because he's under the spotlight. Everyone in the department, from the deputy chief on down to the lowest beat cop, takes orders from Torres."

"I'm sorry you have to babysit us," Heather said.

"Ah, think nothing of it. It's better than tracking down dope dealers on the east side of town. The more time I spend with you, the less chance there is of me having to do something that involves filling out paperwork. I hate doing paperwork."

Heather laughed, and Camay joined her. Hearing the noise,

Olivia got up and joined them in the kitchen.

"What's going on in here?" Olivia asked.

Heather prepared to answer but got interrupted by a knock at the door. She attempted to rise to answer it, but Camay held out a hand and stopped her.

"I got it," Camay said.

Camay stepped to the door, and through the peephole he spotted a woman. He opened the door a crack.

"Yeah?" he said, his voice gruff and off-putting.

"I'm Doctor Trisha Longstreet," the woman said. She produced her ID and held it up to the door.

"Hold on." Camay closed and locked the door. "Olivia, what's the name of that doctor?"

"Trish Longstreet. Why do you ask?"

"Because she's at the door."

"She should have been here about nine hours ago," Heather said.

Camay let the doctor in and escorted her to the kitchen and offered her his chair. Dr. Longstreet sat, put her leather briefcase on the floor, and invited Heather and Olivia to do the same.

"Running a little late, Doc?" Heather said.

"I came by around nine this morning," Longstreet said. "For a good five minutes, I knocked at the door, but no one answered. I left my card under the door with a note that said I'd be back, since I had a full slate of patients today. So, Olivia, would you like to talk?"

"Sure, I guess."

"Great."

Dr. Longstreet retrieved her case, set it on the table and removed a legal pad and a pen from it and placed them in front of her. Before she could ask the question, there was a knock on the door.

Camay moved to the door, hand on his gun as he did. He glanced through the peephole and saw a man in a trucker hat and blue windbreaker. In each hand, he held a large brown paper bag. Camay shoved his gun back into his holster and opened the door.

The delivery man stepped over the threshold and held out a bag, which smelled like fried chicken. "You mind taking this. It's heavy." Without waiting for a response, the delivery man thrust the bag into Camay's chest.

Camay put an arm under the bag so it wouldn't drop to the floor, and when he did, the delivery man put his hand in his coat pocket, found his .380, and pulled the trigger. The report echoed through the house as the bullet passed right through the paper bag and directly into Camay's chest. Camay dropped the bag, looked at the blood spreading across his favorite shirt and dropped dead.

Upon hearing the shot, Heather pushed her chair to get up, then stopped when she looked over and spotted Dr. Longstreet pointing a gun at her.

"Stay where you are," Longstreet said.

Olivia flinched and fought the urge to flee. "What's this about?"

Olivia's body stiffened when she felt a hand fall on her shoulder. The hand tightened on her shoulder, and she tried to squirm away from the pain, but couldn't.

"You never thanked me, Olivia."

He let go of her shoulder, squeezing as hard as he could one last time before he did. She winced as he moved to the kitchen counter. He dropped the brown paper bag he still carried into the sink and removed the gun from his windbreaker pocket. He put his hand in the pocket and shoved a finger through the hole.

"Damn shame. I loved this jacket. Still no thanks, Olivia? Sweet little Olivia."

"For… for what?" Olivia stammered.

"Why, for the booze, of course. You didn't think the vodka fairy provided you with all those bottles, did you?"

"I don't even know you," Olivia said.

"Oh, but I know you. Don't you remember that night we met? That particular Cinco de Mayo? I certainly remember."

"You're Mi… Mi… Michael?" Olivia cried. Tears welled in her eyes, then eventually rolled down her cheeks.

"Michael? Yes. But I've had many names for many women. Ricky, Tommy, Todd, Chuck, Lawrence, James, John, Marc. What's in a name, anyway? Honestly, I've gone by so many, I don't remember what my original name was. Doesn't matter. I'm not that person anymore."

"So, you're Susie's boyfriend?" Heather asked.

"You understand, Susie isn't really Susie, either. Let's see, she's been a Jenna, Ann, Debbie, Lydia, and a DJ. Lots more. Susie is her favorite, though. She loves playing the innocent little victim. Convincing, wasn't she?"

"Then who are you?" Heather asked Dr. Longstreet.

"That's Susie's aunt. She didn't lie about having an aunt she lived with. She just didn't elaborate on any details."

"You're a part of this, too?" Heather asked. "I suppose you have a long list of fake names, too?"

Dr. Longstreet shrugged. "Nope. I'm actually a Trish. Last name is different."

"I'll bet you're not really a doctor," Heather said.
Trish shrugged a second time. "The closest I came to being a doctor was a half a semester in a community college. There's a lot you can do with a print-it-yourself business card and a whole lot of cash. With enough cash, you can fake an entire career if you want to."

"But to what end?" Heather asked. "Why go through all that trouble?"

Michael grinned. "For the game, of course. Susie couldn't play this round, thanks to you, Olivia. But I could. Take your mind and your body from you."

"What do you mean?"

"Messing with the mind was all my idea," Trish said. "I'd

been following your friend Heather for weeks trying to find the right way to get her my business card, and you gave me that gift when you had a little tantrum in that cafe. Then all I needed to do was gain your trust, ask you a few leading questions, and you opened up your little brain to me. All the childhood trauma, the bad relationships. Your fears and your anxieties, and of course, everything you endured at the farmhouse. They loved those videos the best."

"Videos?" Olivia asked.

Michael began laughing hysterically. "Yes! Videos. Everything you told her. Everything was on video. Magnificent picture. Superior sound, and it all played great on our big-screen television. You had your very own television show, and you didn't even know it. We know every one of your secrets and insecurities, and we ate them up like potato chips as we watched you whine and cry over them."

Olivia put her elbows on the table and hid her face in her hands, ashamed.

"That's not all we got."

"What do you mean?" Heather asked.

"Videos of Olivia at home. Boring things, mostly."

"Videos? What videos?" Heather asked.

Michael fished his phone from his pants pocket and fumbled with the screen for a few minutes. He turned the phone around so everyone at the table could see the screen. On it was a frozen image of Olivia lying on her couch. She seemed asleep, her arm hanging over the edge, a bottle of vodka on the floor beside her. Based on the angle, Heather guessed the video was taken from near Nibbler's cage.

Michael started the video. At first, it didn't appear to be playing, but then Olivia lifted her dangling arm and laid it across her chest. The video jerked. Whoever held the camera moved closer to the couch. Soon, the camera stopped right next to the couch, and the image zoomed in on Olivia's face. She faced the back of the couch. Deep in sleep, her eyes moved beneath her lids, and she had a bit of drool coming from the corner of her mouth.

The image shifted as the phone turned around and went into selfie mode. A man appeared in the frame wearing a dark blue stocking cap. He wore dark sunglass to cover his eyes, so only his mouth was visible. The man leaned over until he was cheek to cheek with Olivia. He smiled garishly for the camera, then turned his head and licked Olivia's face from her chin to her hairline.

The video pulled away as the man set the phone on the end table. He stepped into the frame and pulled a knife from his pocket and unfolded it. Slowly, he kneeled next to the couch and gently straightened Olivia's head. He placed his left hand on her forehead and gently pushed her into the couch arm. She weakly struggled for a second, then submitted. The man raised the knife and placed it against Olivia's neck.

"Should I do it?" he whispered to the camera. "Should I end the game and snuff out her light?"

He pressed the knife against her neck and slowly pulled it toward him. Even though he used the knife's spine against her flesh, he pressed hard enough to leave a slight indentation.

"No. Not yet. The game goes on."

The video ended. Michael cleared the screen and shoved the phone in his pocket. "I have more. Dozens more."

The colored drained from Olivia's face, and she shrank into her chair.

Heather glared at Michael, causing him to laugh again.

"Don't look at me. She's the one with the drinking problem," Michael said, pointing at Olivia.

Heather looked at Olivia. Although she wasn't making any noise, Heather could tell by the way her body moved that Liv was sobbing. Olivia shifted in her chair and faced the wall. Heather returned her attention to Michael. There was something about his behavior that seemed odd. They locked eyes for a moment, then Heather had a light come on in her head as she made a connection.

"What did you do?" she asked.

Michael stayed stone-faced for a moment, then broke into a wide grin.

"Olivia never really checked the seals on those bottles. She never noticed I always added a little something extra to help her sleep. To seem more drunk than she actually was. You can thank the drugs, not the booze, for the way she turned out. Between the vodka and what I slipped her, she almost overdosed early on. I had to turn her over so she wouldn't choke on her puke. Since then, once she'd knocked herself out, I dumped the rest of the bottle. Shame, really, wasting all that good vodka."

"Why did you bother saving me at all?" Olivia sobbed.

"Because at that point, it wasn't time for the game to end. You got them?"

"Yes," Trish said. She turned her attention to her briefcase and passed two syringes to Michael.

Michael removed the caps from the first needle and, in a swift motion, stabbed Heather with it and pressed the plunger. She attempted to rise, then fell back into her chair. Michael uncapped the second needle and took a step toward Olivia.

"Don't worry, sweet Olivia. This won't hurt. Much."

CHAPTER TWENTY

Detective Torres pulled up to the safe house at just after one in the morning, angry at having gotten caught up in a wrong lead that ended in a man's death and hours of investigation and paperwork. Caution replaced anger when she exited her car and noticed a delivery vehicle for a local chicken restaurant. The driver's door had a magnetic advertisement that not only gave the name and phone number of the establishment but also the business hours that showed the place had shut down at ten, three hours earlier.

Torres readied her gun and crept to the front door. When she got close enough, she noticed it stood ajar an inch, and light from inside the house streamed out the crack of the door, leaving a pillar of light splayed across the porch.

Holding her revolver ready, she kicked at the bottom of the door, and it swung freely open.

She spotted Camay laying where he'd fallen, back against the wall, chin on his chest, a torn bag at his side, a fried chicken leg half out of the sack. Knowing he was already dead, Torres moved from room to room, searching for anyone else in the house. Five minutes later, she determined she stood alone.

Torres returned to the front door, pulled out her cell, called for backup, and returned to her own car to wait.

Officer Press was the first uniformed officer on scene.

"So that's where it went," he said, getting out of his patrol car.

"Where what went?" Torres asked.

Press pointed at the delivery car. "That. The restaurant reported it stolen two hours ago. The driver is missing, too. Is he in the house?"

"No. Only Corporal Camay. Otherwise, it's empty."
Press took the flashlight from his belt, turned it on, and walked toward the missing SUV. He shined the light in the front windows, then the back.

"Uh, Detective. Could you step over here a moment?"

Torres walked over to the SUV and looked at where the light was shining. The glow highlighted a relaxed hand.

"Aw, damn. Check if the doors are open," she said.

Press leaned over to snag the door handle, but Torres stopped him.

"Forgetting something, Press?" Torres said.

Press looked back at the detective and took the gloves she offered him. He snapped them onto his hands, then attempted to open the rear door, which he found locked. He opened the driver's door, unlocked the rest, and opened the back. Press reached in, checked for a pulse and backed away from the car. "He's dead."

"Is he the delivery driver?" Torres asked.

Press focused his light on the man and pulled his wallet from his back pocket. He handed the wallet to Torres and focused the flashlight on her.

"He's wearing a T-shirt with the restaurant's logo on it, so I think so. What do you think happened here?"

"Come on," Torres said. "Let's check out the house again."

Press followed Torres through the door, turning his head to avoid looking at the dead officer near the front door.

"Take a room and look for anything that might give an indication of what happened here. Don't touch a thing. You find something, call me. Got it?"

Torres started toward the living room while Press made his way to the back of the house. She stepped into the space and, standing in one place, she let her eyes do the searching from where she stood. The room didn't look disturbed, other than the area by the couch. The television remote was on the floor, but it seemed like someone had placed it there. Although there were two throw pillows on the couch, they were both on one end as if someone had taken an afternoon nap.

Once she found nothing abnormal in the living room, Torres moved into the kitchen. There, she stood between the sink and the table and worked through the same exercise. There was a brown bag in the sink, one corner darker than the other, as if something inside had spilled. At the table she noticed table settings for three, but someone had pushed all three haphazardly to the center of the table as if they'd prepared for dinner, then decided not to eat. None of the chairs were pushed in neatly, and one lay on its side.

Torres noticed black marks on the floor. She pulled out her own flashlight and trained the beam on the marks.

"Scuff marks," Torres said.

"What?" Press said as he stepped into the kitchen.

"Someone sitting at this table wore dress shoes."

"Camay had on rubber-soled shoes."

"Good eye, Press. And here I thought you didn't see the body."

"I caught more than enough of it."

"The marks on the floor here are too narrow. A woman's dress shoe made these."

"Someone else was here," Press said. "I doubt that a woman

in high heels offed the delivery driver and got the drop on Camay."

Torres smiled. "You're going to make a brilliant detective someday, Press."

Press smiled. "Thanks. Hey, what's that?" He crouched low and shined the light under the table.

Torres joined him, and she noticed a small card leaning against the baseboard. She took a pen from her pocket, leaned under the table, and pulled the card away from the baseboard and across the floor. From the utensil box, she grabbed a plastic knife and used it to flip the card over.

"Well, I know who was here. Dr. Trisha Longstreet."

* * *

Olivia woke with a headache, with enough light sensitivity that she couldn't fully open her eyes without receiving a stabbing pain in return. She took a few moments, forcing her lids open a little at a time. Olivia lifted her head and took stock of where she was.

"Aw, crap," she muttered as she took in her surroundings.

Olivia looked around, even though moving her head caused her pain. She recognized the place immediately as the kitchen of a long-forgotten mobile home. The kitchen contained no appliances. Someone had piled black trash bags in the space where the fridge once stood. One bag, overfilled with old beer cans, had spilled onto the cheap, avocado green linoleum floor. When she breathed through her nose, Olivia caught the scent of long-spoiled booze.

Several of the cabinets didn't have doors, and those that did were misshapen and didn't fit properly. In one case, the cabinet door hung from a single screw, threatening to let loose at any time.

Olivia's eyes moved to the kitchen door and wondered if it

would open for her. All the glass in the door was missing, replaced with cardboard duct taped into place. She figured there was a window behind her because she could feel a cool breeze on her back. There was another doorway, which Olivia assumed led deeper into the mobile home.

She attempted to move but couldn't. Olivia sighed, not believing she'd gotten into this same situation, in a dirty old kitchen, chained to a chair. This time was different, though. Heather sat across from her, also chained to a chair, still unconscious.

"Heather?" Olivia called.

When Heather didn't respond, Olivia feared the worst.

"Heather!" Olivia screamed.

This time, Heather's chest at least moved, and Olivia breathed a sigh of relief when she saw her friend was still alive.

From the bowels of the mobile home, she heard a bang, and then shuffling noises that got louder as they approached the kitchen. A shadow darkened the doorway, and then Susie shuffled in.

At first, Olivia didn't recognize her. Gone was the Susie that Olivia remembered, with perfect body proportions, long chestnut hair, and eyes to match. The Susie that came into the room looked far different. She'd put on close to fifty pounds. Susie had apparently tried to dye her hair red, but it came out the color of a can of orange soda. She also looked like she'd given herself a haircut with a pair of dull sheep shears. The most noticeable change was the aluminum crutch she had under her right arm. Every time Susie took a step closer, she would drag her right leg behind her.

A slow step and shuffle at a time, Susie made her way to Olivia's side.

Olivia watched with trepidation as Susie crept closer. When she'd gotten to within four feet, Olivia recoiled at the stench coming from Susie. A ripe mixture of body odor combined with indifference.

"Do you see what you did to me?" Susie asked.

Olivia noticed the sneer remained the same. She didn't respond.

"Did you hear me? You did this. You pushed me in that hole. Broke my damn leg. It got infected; you know. If Mitchell didn't find me, I could have died down there."

"Mitchell?" Olivia asked. "Don't you mean Michael?"

"Mitchell, Michael. Who cares? The point is you turned me into this."

Olivia tried to suppress a laugh but couldn't. In response, Susie backhanded Olivia across the face. Olivia's head flew back, hitting the back of the heavy wooden chair behind her. She let out a huff, her eyes opened wide, and she shook her head to clear the stars.

Olivia looked into Susie's eyes. "I did that to you? You don't remember holding me hostage in a silo for over a month? Screw you. Consider yourself lucky. You've gotten less than you actually deserve."

Susie stared at Olivia for a second, then backhanded Olivia again. Olivia's head snapped to the side this time, and she immediately tasted the coppery flavor of blood.

Olivia turned her head and spat in Susie's face.

Susie howled in anger, wiped her face with the bottom of her already-stained T-shirt, and drew her arm back to hit Olivia again.

"Hold on there," Michael said as he entered the room. "You're going about that all wrong. Obviously, she got some spunk back. We have a new player in the game. Let's see how she does, instead."

Michael moved to Heather's side and shook her shoulder. "Hey. Blondie. Wake up."

Heather moaned, but didn't wake.

Michael moved to the cabinets and searched through them

until he found something that would hold water, which turned out to be a yellow plastic ice bucket with the name of a long-defunct motel on the side. He stepped to the sink and turned on the water. At first nothing happened, but then it began to sputter. The faucet groaned, then a yellow-brown liquid only partially resembling water came from the spout. Michael captured a half of a bucket of the rancid water and turned off the tap. He took three casual steps toward Heather, then overturned the bucket, dumping the contents on her head.

Heather sputtered, coughed, and came awake. She blinked, looked around, and tried to discern where she was.

"Finally. She's awake," Michael said. "Welcome to the game."

* * *

Detective Torres owned what she referred to as her 'thinking pencil'. It was Ticonderoga number two. She had never bothered to sharpen it, since she never intended to write with it. Instead, every time she needed to think hard about something, she put the pencil lengthwise between her teeth and gnawed on it like a beaver working on a branch for a dam.

For the last hour, she and Officer Press had worked on tracking down everything they knew about Dr. Trisha Longstreet, which turned out to be a whole lot of nothing.

Torres had woken a judge and got a warrant to search the doctor's office, which was listed on the business card. When they entered the office, they discovered the whole thing was a front. Every file cabinet and drawer in the place was empty. At the receptionist's desk, the computer contained no business files at all. Instead, all it contained was an Internet browser connection, and when Officer Press brought up the history, all he found were links to online games.

Torres took photos of all the degrees and accolades that hung on the wall, and when she got to her office, she worked on verifying everything.

The medical degree was the easiest since the university listed on it didn't exist. The school on the undergraduate degree was real, but there was no sign of a Trisha Longstreet, or any other Longstreet for that matter, actually attending.

Many of the articles of acclaim were fake, and in one case, the fictitious Dr. Longstreet had simply posted her photo over the actual doctor profiled in a magazine article. The second Torres looked at it in the office, she spotted it as a fake, but she realized it would fool someone from a distance.

"I've got something," Officer Press said when he entered Torres' office waving a sheet of paper.

"Tell me," Torres said.

Press put the paper on her desk. "I checked the property records. That farm where they found Olivia Branch? That was originally the property of a man named Taylor. One of the descendants mentioned in his will was a Trisha Taylor."

"So?"

"The person who rented that office did it under a shell company called TriTay. It turns out TriTay owns a couple of other properties in the area. Both abandoned. One's a warehouse, one's a mobile home park."

"My bet is on the mobile home park," Torres said.

Officer Press picked up the paper. "Got the address right here. It's only thirty minutes away."

* * *

Olivia watched helplessly as Michael unchained Heather from the chair and took her to another room. Trish helped him while Susie remained behind to keep an eye on Liv.

"You're going to love this next game," Susie said. "It's one of my personal favorites."

A loud noise came from the other room, getting the attention of Olivia and Susie, who both looked toward the doorway.

Susie gave Olivia a maniacal grin. "He's almost ready for you."

Olivia pulled against the bonds that held her, but unlike the previous time they'd shackled her this way, she didn't have a nail to pick the lock, and the chair seemed so sturdy it wouldn't break. She stopped struggling. For the moment.

Another loud bang came from the living room, this one sounding like a shot from a low-caliber gun. A moment later, Michael entered the room.

"It's time."

* * *

Detective Torres drove slowly through the abandoned mobile home park. Although most of the lots were empty, save random bits of trash and discarded furniture, a few single-wide mobile homes and trailers with flat tires and broken windows dotted the property.

As the detective drove along the muddied ruts that used to be roads, Officer Press looked for signs of life in the buildings.

"Stop!" Press yelled.

Torres stood on the brakes, causing them both to lurch forward in their seats.

"I saw something in that one," Press said, pointing to the rundown home they'd stopped in front of.

Gun drawn; she made her way to the house. The door creaked in the wind, and a tattered once-yellow curtain waved out a broken window.

Torres nodded, and Press opened the door wide, making room for Torres to enter.

The door opened to the living room, which stood empty. To their right stood a kitchen, and to the left was a short hallway.

Torres stood silent, then heard a noise and turned left. Minding her step to not disturb any of the trash which may announce her presence.

She heard voices talking, and she stopped, holding a hand back for Press to let him know to stop, too. Torres used hand singles to countdown from three to one, then she burst into the room.

"Freeze!" Torres screamed the second she stepped over the threshold.

She took a moment to focus as a naked man rolled off of his significant other and put his hands up. The woman he was with grabbed the sleeping bag and tried to hide both her body and her embarrassment.

"I'm not armed!" the man said.

"Yeah, I can see that. Sorry. I've got the wrong place. Carry on."

Torres secured her weapon, and left the house, Press hot her tail.

"Sorry," Press said.

"Don't be." Torres stopped. "Can you see that? Looks like a house in the middle of all those trees?"

"Yeah?"

"I've got a hunch about that one. Let's go."

* * *

Michael led Olivia into the living room, her hands bound in front of her. On the far wall in front of her stood a pool table pushed up onto its short side, pockets facing out. Heather was tied to the table spread-eagle. Ropes extended from the corner pockets, holding her hands, and they'd secured her feet the same way. A rope from the side pockets kept her taut against the table.

"Heather!" Olivia screamed. "Let her go!"

"Tie her down," Michael said to Trish as he pushed Olivia

into an easy chair that expelled a puff of dust when Olivia hit it.

Olivia tensed her body as Trish looped a rope around her, then tied it tight. She tried to shift in the seat but stopped when she got jabbed by several of the broken springs.

"We can't let her go. The game hasn't started yet," Susie said.

She stepped over to a side table on which was a large white plastic bin that said it was the property of the United States Postal Service on the side. She dipped her hand in and brought out a knife and waved it in front of Heather's face. Heather moved her head back and forth, trying to get as far away from the blade as she could, but she had nowhere to go.

Susie stepped back, tossing the knife back into the tub. "You know, Michael saw this knife thrower on the television and got totally obsessed with it. He started throwing knives at everything. Trees, outbuildings, signs. He sucked at first, but he got pretty good. Want to see a demonstration?"

"No," Olivia said. "Let her go."

Michael stepped up to the bin and selected a small paring knife from inside. He positioned himself a few feet in front of Heather and drew his arm back.

"Wait!" Olivia said. "Let her go. Throw the knives at me if you need to."

"No," Susie said. "He can't do that. The name of this game is you watch while he slowly kills your friend."

Before Olivia could object, Michael grunted and threw the knife as hard as he could. Heather screamed and fell silent when the knife stuck in the table six inches above her head.

"You missed," Susie said.

"I was supposed to miss," Michael said. "That's the whole point."

Susie hit Michael in the shin with her crutch. "That's on television, you idiot. We want to kill her."

"Okay. I'll try again."

Michael rooted around in the bin and extracted an all-metal

potato peeler. He waved it in the air for all to see the retro-kitchen tool, complete with its rust stains.

"What's that going to do?" Susie asked.

Michael shrugged, then threw it as hard as he could. It tumbled as it flew through the air, then straightened and flew right into Heather's abdomen, just below her ribcage.

Heather and Olivia screamed as one, one in pain, the other in frustration. The peeler stuck in her and blood streamed from the wound.

"That's more like it!" Susie said. She clapped, then looked into the bin. From it, she pulled a meat cleaver and handed it to Michael. "Try this one next."

Michael spotted movement and turned his head toward the door. "There!"

Everyone turned to look, and they all spotted Officer Press standing in the doorway. Michael threw the knife at the cop, but misjudged the heaviness of it, and it landed near Olivia's feet.

Trish raised her gun and pointed it at the cop, who froze in the moment. As her finger tightened on the weapon, Press fell to the side as Torres pushed him out of the line of fire.

The gun erupted in Trish's hand, and Torres took the bullet in the upper chest. She staggered into the room and fell. Using Olivia's chair as a brace, Torres pulled herself up and returned fire.

CHAPTER TWENTY-ONE

Olivia looked down at Torres' face and noticed the blood draining away. They locked eyes for a moment, then Torres gave Olivia a wink and slid to the floor.

"Michael, that bitch killed my aunt! Get her!" Susie screamed.

Michael moved to Torres. Holding the meat cleaver ready to strike, he used his free hand to move her. Her fixed gaze stared at the ceiling, so he let her fall back. "This one's already dead. I'll check the other one." Michael exchanged the cleaver for the detective's gun.

When Michael left the room, Olivia looked around to determine what else was happening. Susie had moved to her aunt, who had taken Torres' last shot right below the chin. Trish had dropped where she stood.

Olivia looked at her friend. Heather was staring straight ahead, an expression of shock on her face and tears streaming down her cheeks. Olivia glanced at the wound. The potato peeler was still stuck in Heather's side, and based on the steady blood flow, she guessed Michael had managed to nick something important.

Olivia relaxed her body, which loosened the ropes. She squirmed in her chair, trying to find purchase, and had to suppress a scream when she felt something slice her inner thigh. Her hands reached between her legs, and it only took a second to find the broken spring that had cut her flesh.

With her index fingers, Olivia traced the length of the spring and found a burr at the tip. She positioned her hands so that her binding caught the burr and started sawing away. She stopped when Michael entered the room, dragging a handcuffed police officer with him.

"Look what I caught," Michael said. He moved Press over to the wall and kicked him in the stomach.

Press inhaled once and threw up, partially on himself, mostly on Michael's shoes.

"Asshole! Look what you did!" Michael said. He kicked Press again, vomit flying from his shoe as he did, this time twice in the head, and Press stopped moving. Michael wiped his shoe on Press, then turned his attention back to Heather.

Michael's back to her, Olivia resumed cutting through her bindings.

"Are you enjoying this?" Michael said to Heather as he moved closer to her.

"Michael, come over here," Susie screamed. "Come and help her."

Michael shrugged, turned to leave, and pivoted back. He kissed Heather full on the lips. "I'll be right back. Don't go anywhere."

Heather mewed like a cat and sobbed.

Olivia wanted to say some words to comfort her, but didn't want to bring attention to herself, so she remained silent while she sawed away at her ropes.

"What?" Michael said as he reached Susie.

"Help her," Susie whispered. "I think she's still alive."

Michael leaned over the body of Trish Longstreet and took a closer glance. "Are you crazy? That cop blew out half her neck. She's dead."

Susie wailed and beat her fists on Michael's chest. "Do something!"

Michael grabbed Susie's wrists and held them away from him. "You're not hearing me. There's nothing to do."

Angry, Susie clambered to her feet and shuffled to Heather. "I'll tell you what you can do. Take it out on her."

Susie took her crutch, and balancing on her one good leg, swung the crutch like a baseball bat. She caught Heather right in the midsection, and Heather screamed when the potato peeler slipped farther into her body.

Susie's maniacal grin returned, and she drew the crutch back for another swing, but lost her balance and collapsed to the floor. She tried getting up, but couldn't, so she crawled to the side table, dragging her crutch behind her and used the table for support to get back to her feet.

"Michael, get over here."

Michael, who had spent the previous few minutes smirking at Susie's actions, returned to her side.

"Throw something!" Susie said, gesturing at Heather. Michael moved back to the bin, and from it selected a paring knife.

As Olivia watched Michael select another knife, she worked feverishly at her bonds. She took a moment to flex her hands, determined they wouldn't break, and returned to trying to cut through them.

Michael moved only a couple of feet in front of Heather and tossed the knife. It did a single loop through the air, hit flat against Heather's chest, and fell to the floor. He retrieved the knife, moved back to his position, and threw it a second time. Once again, it hit her flat, this time on her left hip, and clattered harmlessly to the floor. Frustrated, Michael picked up the knife and thrust it directly into Heather's left shoulder.

Heather screamed in pain, looked at the knife, and passed out.

"That's no fun," Michael said. He tapped Heather's face a couple of times, and when she didn't respond, he left the room. Olivia paused while he passed, then resumed sawing on her bindings.

Michael returned a minute later carrying the ice bucket full of water, which he dumped over Heather's head. Heather came to for long enough to lift her head an inch and dropped it again.

"Hello?" Michael asked, tapping her face. Not getting a response, Michael pushed Heather's head into the back of the pool table hard enough for everyone in the room to hear the impact of her head against the wood. Still, Heather didn't move.

"I guess we need a little more water," Michael said.

He dribbled the remaining drops of water over Heather's head and rushed back to the kitchen.

The second he passed her; Olivia continued the work on her bonds.

"Hey, what are you doing over there?" Susie asked.

Olivia looked up and noticed Susie stepping toward her. She tested the bindings. They still didn't break, so she returned to sawing at them. Susie was almost on top of her when Olivia tried her bonds one last time, flexed her wrists, and broke through them.

"Damn you!" Susie screamed as she got closer. She swung her crutch at Olivia's head. Olivia raised her hands just in time, caught it, and pushed it backward. Susie took a step back, caught her heel on Torres' arm, and toppled to the floor. Her crutch slid away from her reach, so Susie began crawling after it.

Although her hands were free, Olivia couldn't leave, still tied to the chair. She glanced over the armchair and spotted the meat cleaver sitting on top of the prone body of Detective Torres, right where Michael left it when he traded up for her gun.

Olivia reached as far as she could over the arm but couldn't quite grab the knife. She shifted closer to the side of the chair and screamed when a broken spring pierced her side. Olivia reached for the knife again, and when she noticed how short she was, she changed her tactics, grabbed Torres by the shirt collar, and tried to roll the detective toward her. Her first tug yielded nothing, so Olivia shifted her position again, jabbing the spring deeper into her flesh. Olivia grabbed the detective's collar again, let out a grunt, and pulled. This time, Torres slowly leaned toward Olivia and stopped when she encountered the chair. The cleaver, still an inch too far away, slid closer when Olivia jerked on the shirt.

Meat cleaver in hand, Olivia quickly cut away the ropes that bound her and jumped from the chair. She put a hand to her left side, and when she looked at it, she saw it covered with blood. She absentmindedly wiped the blood on her pants, raised the cleaver, and headed toward Susie, who had finally reached her crutch.

"You stay away from me! Michael! Michael!" Susie screamed.

"What's all the ruckus about?" Michael asked as he stepped into the living room.

Michael spotted Olivia heading toward Susie, cleaver raised and ready to strike. He dropped the ice bucket and pawed at the gun tucked into his belt buckle.

"Stop!" Michael called.

Olivia turned, realized he had the drop on her, and threw the cleaver in Michael's direction. On instinct, Michael stepped to his left to avoid the object, leveling the gun as he did. Just as he pulled the trigger, Officer Press, who had regained consciousness, kicked out with all of his might, contacting Michael's knee and throwing him off-balance. The shot went wide, and hit the wall two feet to Olivia's left, just as Michael tripped and fell.

"Run!" Press yelled.

Not needing further encouragement, Olivia ran in a wide arc to evade Michael's outstretched hand, and then made a dash for the door without looking back.

The first thing Olivia spotted when she left the house was the police car sitting outside. She ran to it, tried the door, and found it locked. Giving up on the car, she did a quick spin to determine what other options she had. She found herself surrounded by trees in three directions, and the remnants of a road on which the car had come in on.

From inside the house, she overheard a yell, which broke Olivia out of her paralysis and she ran into the trees. Unlike her previous escape in the dead of night, the sun seemed almost directly above, which allowed Olivia to scamper over rocks and deadfalls, and pick out the most efficient path as she moved forward.

Olivia stopped for a moment and listened, trying to control her breathing so she might hear something other than her own panting. She caught the crack of wood, as if something heavy had stepped on a brittle branch, but she couldn't discern the direction or the distance. Figuring Michael would easily hear her, she started a slow jog, aware of her footing to make the least possible noise.

Olivia stopped when she came into contact with a barbed-wire fence. Not wanting to deal with the fence, Olivia moved parallel to it. She jogged another hundred yards when she came out of the trees and into a large open tract of land. Off in the distance, she saw a smattering of mobile homes and a couple of RVs. She didn't like the idea of moving out in the open in broad daylight, but not having a choice, Olivia took off for the closest mobile home, hoping they would have a telephone, a gun, or both.

She judged the distance to the mobile home to be three hundred yards, then sprinted as fast as she could across open ground. After she'd covered half the distance, Olivia stopped and bent over, trying to catch her breath. Her hand went to her fresh wound and discovered she was still bleeding.

"Shit," Olivia said, still gasping for air as she stood straight. Realizing Michael could spot her at any time, she started walking toward the mobile home as fast as she could without feeling winded. She'd almost made it to the door when she heard the report of a gun behind her.

Olivia turned around and noticed Michael at the tree line from where she'd just come.

"I see you!" Michael yelled.

Olivia barely caught the words but got herself into gear when Michael started running toward her.

Olivia arrived at the door to the mobile home, knocked on it, and got a surprise when the door opened freely. She moved into the room, and it took her only a second to realize it was abandoned. The room was a mess, covered in mounds of trash. Graffiti artists had done a number on the interior, and spray paint cans littered the room like hot dog wrappers blowing in the wind at a county fair.

She rushed to the kitchen to find anything that she could use as a weapon, but that room looked completely gutted right down to the frame. Only the cheaply tiled floor and a remnant of wallpaper told Olivia that it had once functioned as a kitchen. The room was also missing part of the outer wall. Rather than explore the rest of the house and lose time in the process, Olivia picked her way carefully through the hole and set her hopes on the next mobile home, which was only fifty yards ahead.

"Olivia! I'm coming!" Michael screamed.

The voice seemed much closer, so despite the hitch in her chest from her aching ribs and her new wound, Olivia took off at a full run, then slowed to a jog when she found herself short of breath.

"Olivia!" Michael yelled again.

She felt he was almost upon her, so she turned to look

behind. When she did, she ran into a pipe she hadn't seen, tripped, and fell hands-first onto the rocky and weed-infested ground. Ignoring the pain in her hands, Olivia turned around and found Michael had not discovered where she was. Wanting to keep the advantage, Liv scrambled to her feet and ran the rest of the way to the house.

When she arrived at the door, she expected it would open just as easily as the previous one, but to her surprise, it was locked. She threw her shoulder against the door, and although it rattled in the frame, it didn't yield to her.

Olivia backed away from the mobile home and did a quick spin. Other than the one Michael ran for, this was her only shot at safety without having to run farther across open terrain. She knew she didn't have the physical capacity for it.

"Okay, Olivia. Work the problem. Work the problem. Door clearly locked. Look for an open window or another door," she said to herself.

She descended the stairs from the door and moved to the first window. She reached up, realizing that even if it were unlocked and wide open, she wouldn't be able to boost herself into it. Olivia kept moving around the house, hoping to find a lower window, something to climb on, or another door. She walked around the entire building and ended back at the front stoop.

"Olivia! I see you!" Michael shouted.

She turned around and spotted him inside the hole in the wall she'd climbed out of. When she spun back around to attempt the door again, she caught her foot on the well-weathered welcome mat.

"There can't be…"

Olivia bent and lifted the corner of the mat. The weathered corner came apart in her hand, leaving a pile of crumbling rubber in her palm. She let the debris fall between her fingers. When she looked down, she saw the teeth of a bronze key. Olivia picked the key from the ground, placed it in the lock, and opened the door. She stepped over the threshold, closed the door behind her, and took a half step when she realized most of the living room floor was missing.

From her perspective, it appeared someone had ripped out the under flooring to use for something else and left a gaping hole in its place. Only Olivia's short stride had saved her from going too far and falling four feet to the hard earth underneath.

"Olivia! Come play with me!" Michael called. He sounded too close for comfort.

She overheard him shuffle up the concrete stairs, then the doorknob rattled.

Michael knocked gently on the door. "Little pig, let me in."

Olivia didn't answer.

Michael pounded on the door. "Come on. I saw you go in there. You can't hide from me."

When Olivia failed to answer again, a brief silence was followed by a slam at the door. Olivia knew Michael was trying to break his way in, just like she had done at first.

BAM! Michael shouldered the door again. Olivia held her breath.

BAM! Michael hit the door a third time. The frame rattled but held.

BAM! Michael hit the door a fourth time, and a crack appeared in the wood.

Olivia counted to three, and on that count, unlocked and opened the door. Michael was already moving toward it, shoulder down, expecting resistance. With nothing to block his way, Michael stumbled into the room, stepped on the edge of the flooring, and tumbled headfirst into the hole.

Olivia detected a sickening crunch, then stepped to the edge and carefully peered in. The angle of Michael's head told her she'd never have to worry about him again.

In a closet, Olivia found an empty five-gallon pail that used to hold paint. She dropped it into the hole, then lowered herself in. Michael had fallen with the gun under him, so she needed to flip his body over to access it. After a few moments, gun in hand, Olivia stood on top of the inverted bucket to give her the boost she needed to get out of the hole.

Once out in the sunshine, Olivia removed the magazine and counted the number of bullets. Satisfied she had enough to finish the job, she started the walk back to get Heather.

It took only seven minutes to return to the original mobile home. She walked in the kitchen door without hesitation, then passed right into the living room. When she entered, she noticed Heather had a knife sticking out of her left thigh, and Susie was preparing to add a fourth.

"Get away from her," Olivia ordered.

Susie turned around and saw Olivia. "Where's Michael?"

"Michael's dead," Olivia stated in an icy tone.

"That, that can't be," Susie said.

"Why not?"

Susie lurched forward a step, and then another. She held up the knife and thrust it in Olivia's direction, even though she was still a foot out of reach.

"Because, sweet Olivia. That's not how we play the game!"

"Well, I've got some terrible news for you," Olivia said.

"What?"

"The game is over, bitch."

Olivia raised the gun and fired off one shot. It caught Susie in the center of her chest, and she dropped to the ground without another word.

<h1 style="text-align:center">EPILOGUE</h1>

Officer Press knocked on the office door of Dr. James Seer and poked his head in.

Dr. Seer was on the phone but waved the officer in and pointed to the guest chair in front of his desk.

Having never been in the room before, Press took an opportunity to look around. On a bookshelf filled with medical texts, he spotted a picture. He rose from the chair, moved to the case, and picked up the frame to take a closer look. In the picture, a much younger James Seer stood next to a much younger Gloria Torres. Both wore baseball uniforms. The front of James's shirt was streaked with dirt. Gloria's shirt was clean. Press sensed the doctor's approach.

"Didn't she play? I can't imagine she would be someone to ride the bench."

"She played. The best pitcher on the team. Never lost a game," James said.

"You understand she saved my life," Press said, a bit louder than a whisper.

"I heard."

"You knew her a long time, right?" Press asked.

James smiled. "Just about forever."

Press put the photograph back where he found it. "I'm sorry she's gone."

James moved back to his chair and sat. "My wife is due to deliver our daughter in a couple of months. We've already agreed to name her Gloria."

* * *

Olivia stepped into the kitchen. "Want tea or coffee?" she asked.

"I'll take a Dr. Pepper if you have one."

Olivia opened the fridge, found two cans, and placed them on the kitchen island. "Want ice? Or a glass?"

"No."

Olivia opened both cans and slid one to her friend. They toasted with the cans, then drank.

"Want to play some cribbage?" Olivia asked.

"Sure. How's Heather doing?"

"Not too bad. She recovered nicely from her physical wounds, but she's still got a long way to go mentally."

"It's great of you to take care of her like this."

"Why wouldn't I? She watched over me for almost a year."

Olivia went to the fridge and pulled from it a cheese and sausage tray. She placed it on the island, then from it selected a thin slice of sausage and a cube of cheddar. Olivia moved across the living room and spotted Nibbler sleeping in his hamster wheel.

"Hey, buddy."

Nibbler woke at the sound of her voice and perked up when he saw Olivia. He left the wheel, moved to the front of his cage, and stood on his hind legs; tiny mouse paws extended in the air.

He squeaked excitedly. Olivia leaned in and gave him the sausage, and then the cheese. Nibbler placed both on the cage floor and extended his paws again. Olivia took a few moments to scratch him between the ears and headed back to the kitchen.

She took a seat and picked up the cards dealt to her. She scanned them briefly, selected two, and tossed them into the crib.

"I understand you're going to get your thirty-day chip soon."

"Tuesday," Olivia said.

"I'm so proud of you."

Olivia smiled, and her cheeks reddened. "Thank you. I've still got a long way to go."

Olivia set her cards face down on the island in front of her. "I'm so sorry I treated you the way I did. I harbored a lot of anger toward you for a long time, and I know what happened to me was never your fault. It was their fault."

"You've already apologized. Several times. I understand how hard the whole thing has been."

Olivia rose from her chair, kissed her friend on the cheek, and drew her into a hug.

"I love you, Sarah."

"I love you, too, Liv."

ABOUT THE AUTHOR

Dan DeKoning was born and raised in Milwaukee, Wisconsin, and currently lives in Knoxville, Tennessee with his wife and their cats.

He is a storyteller and poet who loves to write in a variety of genres and themes. He is also a voracious reader who loves to read anything he can get his hands on.

When he's not writing, you can find him hunting for treasures in used bookstores, or out exploring the planet, or geocaching, or searching for adventures and stories to tell.

Check out his website at www.dandekoning.com.

BIBLIOGRAPHY

Fiction
Déjà Vu
The Haunting of Hyacinth House
How Deep the Darkness
Baker's Crossing

Geocaching Mystery Series
The Cacheland Conspiracy
The Quincy Bay Quandary
The Secret of the Seven Valleys
The Geocaching Mystery Omnibus – Volume 1

Codi Cassidy Cozy Mystery Series
Acoustics and Alibis
Ballads and Bloodshed
Codas and Calibers
Codi Cassidy Mystery Omnibus – Volume 1

Non-fiction
The Geocaching County Tracker

Poetry Collections
Lost and Found
Random Thoughts